T

Red's nostrils flared, which almost looked comical on such a slight man. He held the gun in front of him, leveling it at Clint's head . . . .

"Is that all you want?" Clint asked. "To be the man who kills me . . . like this?"

"I'll be famous. Then rich."

"You'll be remembered like Bob Ford. A pathetic little man who shot a famous one in the back. If he'd killed Jesse in a fair fight, that might have been different."

Red's finger was tensing on the trigger, making the barrel of his gun waver slightly in Clint's face. One twitch was all he needed. "You sayin' you want a fair fight?"

"No. I want to handle my business here and leave. But if you want fame, you won't get it this way."

Red thought it over and made his decision, a thin smile sneaking over ratlike features. "I'll take my chances with fame," he said, "but not with you."

Clint knew he had less than a second to dodge the bullet . . . .

DON'T MISS THESE ALL-ACTION WESTERN SERIES FROM THE BERKLEY PUBLISHING GROUP

THE GUNSMITH by J. R. Roberts

Clint Adams was a legend among lawmen, outlaws, and ladies. They called him . . . the Gunsmith.

LONGARM by Tabor Evans

The popular long-running series about U.S. Deputy Marshal Long—his life, his loves, his fight for justice.

SLOCUM by Jake Logan

Today's longest-running action Western. John Slocum rides a deadly trail of hot blood and cold steel.

BUSHWHACKERS by B. J. Lanagan

An action-packed series by the creators of Longarm! The rousing adventures of the most brutal gang of cutthroats ever assembled—Quantrill's Raiders.

DIAMONDBACK by Guy Brewer

Dex Yancy is Diamondback, a southern gentleman turned con man when his brother cheats him out of the family fortune. Ladies love him. Gamblers hate him. But nobody pulls one over on Dex . . .

WILDGUN by Jack Hanson

Will Barlow's continuing search for his daughter, kidnapped by the Blackfeet Indians who slaughtered the rest of his family.

J. R. ROBERTS

JOVE BOOKS, NEW YORK

DEADLY BUSINESS

A Jove Book / published by arrangement with
the author

PRINTING HISTORY
Jove edition / June 2001

For information address: The Berkley Publishing Group,
a division of Penguin Putnam Inc.,
375 Hudson Street, New York, New York 10014.

The Penguin Putnam Inc. World Wide Web site address is
http://www.penguinputnam.com

ISBN: 0-515-13066-4

A JOVE BOOK®
Jove Books are published by The Berkley Publishing Group,
a division of Penguin Putnam Inc.,
375 Hudson Street, New York, New York 10014.
JOVE and the "J" design
are trademarks belonging to Penguin Putnam Inc.

PRINTED IN THE UNITED STATES OF AMERICA

10 9 8 7 6 5 4 3 2 1

ONE

To most of the people who lived there, Wayne, Nebraska, was the biggest town this side of Omaha. It had plenty of water, a hotel, and even a new saloon thanks to a prospector who'd hit it rich out west and come home to settle. Soon, there would be a dry goods store next to the lot, which functioned well enough as a livery.

To Clint Adams, Wayne wasn't much more than a glorified camp. There seemed to be plenty of people milling about, but not much else besides two buildings and lots of tents held up by wooden frames. One of those tents had a sign hung from its front post declaring itself a saloon and there seemed to be a place to hitch Eclipse, which were two reasons good enough for Clint to climb out of the saddle and give his legs a stretch.

The street was nothing more than a piece of trail that had been widened out and heavily rutted. There were about five or six structures on either side of the dirt path and a few more scattered on the outskirts of town. The two wooden buildings were a hotel and a two-level house at the far end of the street. Since Clint didn't care who the rich folks of Wayne were and wasn't planning to stay long enough to need a hotel room, he ignored the buildings and headed straight for the saloon.

After walking Eclipse to the hitching post outside the large tent, Clint tied him off and scratched his neck. The Darley Arabian stallion nudged his hand before dipping his head to drink from a leaky trough that looked like it was used more by drunks than horses. As if to prove that theory, a chewed-up wide-brimmed hat floated to the surface as soon as it was disturbed by Eclipse's snout. Clint fished out the hat, chucked it to the ground, and headed inside.

Judging by the fairly well constructed wood frame, the entrance to the saloon used to have a door instead of a canvas flap. Ducking to clear the frame, Clint stepped inside and quickly found the door had been laid over a pair of wooden posts, where it was nailed down and used as a bar. He walked up to the only empty space, squeezing himself between a pair of cowboys who smelled worse than the animals they drove, and knocked on the door for service.

The bartender was a man so skinny it looked like the dirt on his face was the only thing holding him together. A few days' growth obscured his features even more, but was unable to hide the glint in his small, dark eyes.

"Come in," the bartender said by way of finishing the joke.

"What's the specialty of the house?" Clint asked.

"Whatever fell off the wagon when it passed through. Since no wagons ain't been through here lately, today's special is 'shine." Slapping a glass down over a small bullet hole, the bartender bent down to pull a large jug from beneath the table. "Good part is it was made fresh yesterday mornin'."

Clint reached for the glass when his hand accidentally bumped against something sticking out of the bar. Whether it was there as a statement of character or forgetfulness, the door's thin, rusted handle hadn't been removed from the wood. That explained why the space was empty.

"Name's Edgar," the bartender said as he tipped the jug. When he poured, the potent smell of grain alcohol drifted into Clint's nose, overpowering all of the other odors in the room. Considering the company, that wasn't an entirely bad thing.

Clint took the glass and tossed it back, knowing he'd never get the liquid down if he took the time to think it over. Although the 'shine burned a hot trail to Clint's stomach, the feeling wasn't altogether unpleasant. Still, he couldn't keep his face from twisting.

Edgar was looking on with a friendly smile. "That'll take the edge off a long day, won't it?"

"I think this stuff would take the edge off a hunting knife, but I'm not complaining."

"Set you up with another?"

Standing at the bar, Clint felt as though he'd been riding for weeks. As the shot of alcohol made its rounds through his system, it also burned the taste of dust from his mouth. "Actually, I think I'll take you up on that."

"We sure don't get a lot of strangers through Wayne," Edgar said as he poured another healthy dose. "Tell you the truth, I can't say as I mind seein' a new face around here. Where you headed?"

Clint held on to his glass, this time only taking a sip from the top. "Thought I'd head up north to Minnesota. There's some friends there who I haven't seen for a while, and I thought I'd check up on them."

"Never been up that far. Maybe you'll let me know if it's worth a trip when you head over here on your way back."

Clint nodded and leaned forward, resting his elbows on the bar. Just then, someone called Edgar to the back of the room and the spindly little man set the jug carefully on the floor before rushing to a group of men sitting at one of the saloon's three tables. Relaxing while nursing his drink, Clint eased the cramps from his neck and shifted his feet.

In truth, he was headed up to South Dakota for a high-stakes poker game being run by an old rancher he'd met in West Texas. Clint had found out more than once that telling strangers where he was going usually didn't amount to anything good.

Sometimes, Clint thought it might not be so bad to spend his life in a town where he could live as someone besides The Gunsmith. He took another sip from his drink while the plans started to form.

With all his experience, he could open one hell of a saloon, complete with gaming tables and monthly poker tournaments. He could spend his days relaxing for a living and hang his gun behind the bar. After awhile, when he got bored, he could ride to another town and set up shop there after selling off his old place for a healthy profit.

That didn't sound bad at all. Especially when compared to the life of someone who had a target painted on his back for those looking to make a name for themselves by gunning him down.

Before he knew it, Clint had finished off his drink and was feeling the itch to get moving. It was that itch, he knew, that would always keep him away from any type of quiet life. Besides, he didn't have much of a mind for business.

Setting his glass onto the bar, Clint stepped over to where Edgar was standing. The bartender seemed to be engaged in a heated conversation about one of the drunk's bar tabs. At first, Clint kept his distance and let Edgar handle his own affairs. Then something seemed to strike Clint as being out of place.

It wasn't the words being spoken or even the angry voices being used. The bartender seemed to be doing his best to keep the peace without backing down, but there was something about the men at the table that didn't seem right. Clint watched the drunks closely and found what had been bothering him.

Although all four men at the table slurred their words and ranted like drunks, none of them seemed to move like drunks. Their eyes didn't waver from Edgar. Their shoulders were squared off and their muscles were tensed. Their hands were steady . . . even as two of them snuck their guns from their holsters and cocked them under the table.

Clint's hand drifted to his pistol, amazed at how quickly he'd been punished for even thinking about the quiet life.

TWO

"After all the money we spent in this shit hole you want to cheat us out of more?" raged the drunk who seemed to be the spokesman for his group.

Edgar held his hands out defensively in front of him, but didn't back away. "I ain't tryin' to cheat you out of anything you don't owe, Red. You and your boys there have been coming in here every night for well into a week, and you ain't paid for nothing since your first round."

Red was not a big man, but compared to Edgar, he was big enough to stand up and stare defiantly at the bartender. His narrow shoulders were hunched forward, and his arms reached out to grip the side of his table. Sunken eyes narrowed until they were almost shut beneath a hat that didn't look much better than the one that had been floating in the trough outside. "Now you're sayin' I'm a bum, is that it?"

Clint recognized the deadly intent that had crept into Red's tone and decided he liked Edgar just enough to keep him from getting shot. "I think all the man's asking is for you to settle your bill," he said as he stepped up next to the barkeep.

Turning his eyes toward the new voice, Red looked at Clint as though he was about to spit. "So who the hell are you?"

"Someone who pays for his drinks," Clint said as he dropped a coin into Edgar's shirt pocket.

The three other men at the table looked to Red as if waiting for orders. Every one of them seemed sober and ready to move. Red kept his eyes on Clint, not needing to look back to know his men were there and waiting. "Now's your chance to walk away," Red said. "It's not something I give everyone."

"Funny, but that's what I was about to say to you."

The saloon had been filled with voices and the sound of fists slamming against wood, but now it was deathly quiet. Every eye was on the table in back, either in fear or simply waiting for the day's entertainment.

"Is this bill of yours big enough to die for?" Clint asked.

Red stared into Clint's eyes, and what he saw there made him change his tune. Though at least two of his men had their guns already drawn and held beneath the table, he decided not to chance it.

"Put the guns away," he commanded, even though to an observer none of his men had been fast enough to clear leather. "Looks like ol' Edgar hired himself some protection."

"No, no . . ." the barkeep protested. "All I want—"

Clint silenced him with a touch on the shoulder. "What's this about? You're not drunk, and you're not very good actors. I know this is a small town, but you can't be bored enough to gun down an unarmed man for no good reason."

"Oh, we got reason."

Clint was about to press for more when something caught his attention. If the place hadn't been so quiet, he might not have heard the sound of a well-oiled hammer clicking into place. As it was, the sound of the gun was unmistakable and echoed in his ears like the crack of a whip.

With the other three men still sitting, it was hard to tell which of them was getting ready to fire. Instead of standing still long enough to figure it out, Clint shoved Edgar to one side while he dove to the other. Holes were blown through the table as if the wood itself had decided to explode, sending a rain of splinters into the air where Clint had been only half a second before.

Clint ducked low and spun around to face Red as the other three men overturned the table and got to their feet. A shorter guy with a full beard and the build of a scarecrow stood to Red's left. He was the only one with a gun in his hand, and he was also the only one to be blown from his feet when Clint returned fire. The only thing saving the rest of the table was their common sense.

"Hold it, hold it!" Red hollered as he threw his empty hands out in front of him. He didn't even really have to issue the command. "I told you to put up your guns!"

Seeing they were out of their league, the two men next to Red froze with their hands in midair.

Clint kept his weapon aimed at the group. "Take those guns from them, Edgar."

The barkeep took a tentative step toward the men, being careful not to trip over the body at their feet. The only one not to grumble a threat or take a halfhearted swing as they were disarmed was Red. He kept his eyes on Clint the whole time.

"So who's paying you?" Clint asked.

Red just smirked and shook his head.

Looking over to Edgar, Clint made sure none of the men at the table were feeling brave enough to start something with the reedy little barkeep. Once all the guns were gathered, he holstered his own.

"Now wasn't that easy?" Clint asked. "Everything doesn't have to be as hard as it was for your friend on the ground there."

Edgar looked over to Clint with his hands full of pistols. He backpedaled from the table and headed behind his overturned door. Carefully, he set the guns down into a pile. "What're you gonna do with 'em now?"

"I'll wait here and keep them company while you get your sheriff," Clint said.

"Sheriff? We ain't got no law here yet, mister. Town ain't big enough."

Shrugging, Clint turned and started walking out of the saloon. "Well, I guess you'll just have to toss them out yourself. I won't stand by and watch a murder, but I'm not staying here to nursemaid this bunch, either."

Clint was about to peel away the flap covering the entrance when he heard a voice shouting at his back.

"What about this man that you killed?" Red asked.

Clint stopped with his hand on the canvas, paused, and then looked over his shoulder. "You can put that one's drinks on my tab." He opened the flap and took a refreshing breath of air. Letting the material fall back into place, he unhitched Eclipse and mounted up. He could already hear excited voices coming from the other side of the canvas tent as the stallion made his way down the middle of the street.

"Mister!" came a familiar voice from behind. "Mister . . . wait!"

Pulling back on the reins, Clint slowed down as he listened to footsteps slapping against the mud. The weather was hot and just humid enough to keep the moisture in the ground, making the streets sticky and the mud smell like the underside of a rotted log. All of this combined made it seem like forever before Edgar caught up to him. Already Clint could feel his clothes sticking to his back.

"What is it Edgar?" Clint asked without looking at the lanky man. "I think I've had enough of your town and its welcoming committee."

By the time Edgar caught up, his boots were coated in mud. "I need to talk to you. It's real important," the barkeep said. "At least let me buy you a meal to thank you for what you did."

"Not interested."

"But those men will be back! I know they will."

Clint brought Eclipse to a stop and glanced down. "What you need is some law in this town. I'm not interested in taking on all your local riffraff, and I don't wear a badge. This place got along fine before I got here, and it'll do fine after I leave. Now, if you'll excuse me, I've got a long trail ahead of me." Tipping his hat, Clint nudged Eclipse with his heels.

The stallion hadn't made it twenty feet before he was once again reined to a stop. Letting out a heavy sigh, Clint jumped from the saddle and led Eclipse back to where Edgar was standing.

The barkeep hadn't moved. With the condition of the road, it might have been because his boots were stuck. Judging by the surprise on his face, he most certainly wasn't expecting Clint to come back.

"All right," Clint said. "Why don't you buy me something to eat, and we'll be even."

"Sure, mister, sure!" Edgar said as he led Clint toward the

hotel. "A meal's the least I can do. While we eat, I can tell you why I came for ya in such a rush."

"I'm sure you will," Clint said as he tied Eclipse to a large post in front of the hotel.

THREE

The hotel was run by the same man who lived in the nicest home in Wayne, Nebraska. Apparently Karl Dolffmann didn't like big cities, but he didn't want to live in a tent either. His hotel had high hopes. With ten rooms and a dining area big enough to feed most of the town, The Wayne Lodge was almost grand enough to take Clint's mind away from the fact that he had allowed himself to be lured off the trail.

He and Edgar sat at a table near a window in the middle of the lunchtime rush. The rest of the crowd consisted of two families of three and five, respectively and an old woman sitting by herself at a table in the corner. Their food was in front of them in less time than it took for Clint's stomach to growl.

"This is the best place in town," Edgar said while rubbing his hands together. He'd ordered potato stew, which he attacked as though it was his last meal.

Clint couldn't keep his eyes from widening when the thickest cut of steak he'd ever seen was dropped on the table in front of him with a heavy thunk. Suddenly, campfire cooking didn't seem so attractive anymore. Edgar had been good enough to hold his story until the food came, but looked like he was going to bust if he didn't get it off his chest.

"So who were those men at your saloon, Edgar?" Clint asked before the barkeep exploded.

"Red and all his boys is from around here."

"You said you needed to tell me something?"

"What I wanted to say was that, even if you got those fellas to get out of here and leave town for good, there'd just be another set come down before too long anyway."

Clint was sopping up some of the steak juices with a freshly baked roll. Before he could think it, a fresh beer was set down to replace the one he'd already finished off. "That just brings me back to what I was saying before. You need law in this town, not me."

"But this trouble don't come from Wayne, mister . . ." Suddenly, Edgar turned his face away and started to laugh. "Where the hell are my manners? I don't remember your name."

"It's all right. I never gave it." Reaching across the table, Clint introduced himself. Almost immediately Edgar turned whiter than the tablecloth.

"Clint Adams? I heard'a you. You're The Gunsmith."

"Mind keeping your voice down? I'm not a big fan of advertising."

Flustered, Edgar wiped his hands on his shirt and finally shook the hand Clint had offered. Although he was loud enough, nobody else in the place seemed to care too much about what Edgar was saying. Either they were ignoring him or the folks in Wayne just kept to their own affairs.

"Sorry, Mister Adams. It's just that I couldn't have asked for someone better than you to help me out."

"I'm just passing through town," Clint said. "I've had to shoot one man already, so I think that's about all the help I'm willing to give."

"That's something else I wanted to talk to you about."

Clint didn't like the sound in Edgar's voice. There was bad news brewing behind those words. "Go on."

"I wasn't about to try and stop you, but you really need to stay until we square that away."

"Square what away? That man would have killed us both if I hadn't cleared the path for the bullet. You know it. Everyone in that saloon knows it. Besides, who am I supposed to square things with? You said this town didn't have any law."

"Well, we still have a way of dealing with things."

At the moment, no matter how good the food was, Clint was losing his desire to spend any more time in Wayne. "Look,

I let you turn me around and come back here, so why don't you start making it worth my while before I change my mind again."

Edgar shifted uncomfortably in his seat. "I ain't tryin' to threaten you none. You just need to talk to old man Jorgens. He's the undertaker. Other than that, you're free to go, but what I was startin' to say is that there'll be plenty more bodies in Jorgens's parlor when the next batch of killers come ridin' in to burn me out."

Clint finished off his steak and took the last draw of his beer. A girl in her late teens came by to clear everything off less than a minute later. "No offense, Edgar, but nothing in this town seems big enough to be worth the fuss of hiring guns to take any of it out. Why would anyone want to do that?"

"That's just it, Mister Adams. I don't have the faintest idea why someone would come after me. All I know is that they've been coming for the last month or so. And I ain't the only one, either. Just about every other business in Wayne is on their way out. Hell, last week alone the dry goods store folded up and left, taking the town doctor and Mark Farrell with 'em."

"Let me guess," Clint said. "Everyone is scared for their business here except for the guy that owns this hotel, right?"

"Mark Farrell used to own this hotel. He had the most money of anybody in town. Now the German's runnin' it, and his wife does the cooking."

"Well she does one hell of a job." Clint leaned back to give his food some room to digest. Usually it was the men with the money who did most of the pushing in situations like these. If the rich guy had already been run out of town, who had been the one to force him out? Shaking his head, Clint tried to get himself ready to leave this little camp and their little troubles behind.

"I'm sorry about all your problems," Clint said. "But I don't know what I'm supposed to do about them." He didn't like standing by and watching others get their livelihood taken from them, but then again, Clint couldn't take on the world's problems either. Something about this whole situation bothered him. There was something else that bothered him more, however.

Namely, the smoke rolling out from the kitchen and the

sound of roaring flames coming from the direction of the lobby.

Clint got to his feet at the same time as everyone else in the dining room. The few other diners stampeded outside in a blind panic. Edgar had started toward the door, but held his ground, unsure of what he was going to do next. In the lobby, Clint could see flames licking the front desk, and it wouldn't be long before the way outside was blocked by a wall of fire.

"Maybe we should take this outside," Clint calmly said as he motioned for Edgar to go ahead of him.

They all jogged for the door. When Clint stepped outside, he looked for Eclipse. The stallion was still tied to his post and was anxious to leave, but fine otherwise. The town, on the other hand, was a different story.

Apparently, everything that could hold a spark had been set ablaze.

FOUR

The first thing Clint thought to do was loosen Eclipse's reins and lead him away from the burning hotel. The big stallion reared instinctively, but kept his head long enough to be taken safely away. With his circus background, the Darley Arabian had probably seen his fair share of fire, but nothing on this scale. Once he got near the livery, there was already a group of boys ready to take his reins.

"Don't worry, none," one of the older ones said. He had to shout to be heard over the ruckus that had erupted. "We got a place for 'em well away from the fire!"

Clint handed over Eclipse's reins and ran toward the nearest tent, where there was already a group of townspeople frantically stripping away the canvas. Looking over his shoulders as he lent his muscle to the effort, he saw that everybody who was able was doing their part to find a spot on the rough material that wasn't on fire so they could pull it down before the wooden frames were lost as well.

Luckily, none of the tents on this side of the town were bigger than a small shack, and it didn't take the men long to pull down the canvas and stomp their boots onto the flames until the fire was smothered by the mud. Although most of the tarp was lost, the frame along with just about everything inside had been saved from being reduced to ashes.

No sooner had the smoke started to curl into the air than

everyone ran over to the next tent. The fire had had more time to take hold by the time they got there, but a group was already working to tear down the canvas, which seemed to be stuck on the top corner of one of the wooden support posts.

Clint ran past a young mother who was shielding an infant. They were well out of the reach of the fire and were soon noticed by a larger group of men who'd been fighting the blaze.

Everything was happening so fast, Clint barely had a moment to survey the extent of the damage before he was swept along to help disassemble another tent. Each one he did was harder than the next. Thankfully, there were plenty of other groups working as fast as they could. Clint came to another, bigger structure, and realized he'd made it all the way back to Edgar's saloon.

The roar of the flames was still a constant rumble in his ears, but it had eased up considerably once the entire town had sprung into action. Standing at the front of the saloon, Clint heard a rush of footsteps coming from the other side of the large tent, followed quickly by the crack of wood and a blast of heat.

Edgar, who Clint hadn't seen since running from the hotel, led a group of men around the saloon. All their faces were blackened with soot, and Edgar's hands were blistered and bloody.

Spotting Clint, the barkeep ran over to him and started tugging the canvas from the door frame. "I rushed over here as soon as I could," Edgar said as he struggled with hooks and nails that sizzled when he touched them, frying his skin on contact.

Running on impulse, Clint grabbed hold of a portion of canvas and started pulling it free of its wooden support. Pieces of material came away in his hands. Wood from the frame broke off in brittle chunks and the heat from the flames was only getting hotter. Clint could feel his arms and hands blistering as smoke crawled up into his nose and down his throat, making it harder for him to breathe.

Soon, all he could see were vague outlines and blobs moving through the haze. Voices were blending with the crackling roar and before long, all he could hear was the fire as it crept closer to him with every passing second. One voice in particular started to distinguish itself from the racket, although he still couldn't make out any exact words.

Just as the heat began to rise even further, Clint was pulled away from the canvas in time to watch it ignite. The fire had made it from the back of the saloon all the way around to the front. In fact, the part of the door where Clint had been standing was quickly engulfed in flames.

Only after the entire place was burning did Clint realize he was being dragged across the street where the fire had been all but snuffed. The smoke was still thick in the air, but a strong breeze whipped over the entire town, which was both a blessing and a curse. While it brought fresh air to breathe, it also fanned the flames that were left.

"You all right?" came a haggard voice from directly behind.

Clint tried to turn, but found he was still being held back. When he started struggling, they quickly let go, and he was free to move. Standing behind him was a large bear of a man wearing coveralls and a simple wide-brimmed hat. Next to the big man was Edgar. Both were covered head to foot in thick layers of soot, mud, and painful looking heat blisters. If the way he felt was any indication, Clint looked just as bad.

"You look like hell," Edgar said in confirmation.

Clint felt as though he'd been mule-kicked in the head. His eyes burned, and the world seemed to swirl and waver around him. His feet were unsteady, and his mouth tasted like the bottom of a stove. Just as he thought he would fall over, the two men grabbed hold and lowered him to the ground, plopping themselves down heavily on either side.

"You took in a lot of that smoke," the bigger man said as he leaned back against an exposed wooden pole and wiped the black from his eyes. "It'd be best for you to rest for a spell, or you'll keel over."

Although he doubted he had the energy to stand, Clint began trying to lift himself up. "That saloon is still on fire," he said weakly. "I can help."

Clint managed to get one foot beneath him before the other man's huge palm slapped him back down to a sitting position.

When the burly townsman spoke, he had to pause to hack up black crud and spit it on the ground. "Too late . . . it's gone—" Another coughing spell. "You did plenty. Just rest for a bit."

Edgar, who'd been quiet until now, leaned forward with his head on his knees and watched his business burn to the ground. "Hank's right," the barkeep said without turning away from the fire. "My place must've been set on fire first. That and the hotel. We tried to save it, but there's not a lot we can do. . . ."

When Edgar's voice trailed off, Clint felt his senses returning bit by bit. He looked around and saw that the little settlement had been mostly disassembled and reduced to a smoking patch in the mud. People were running about like mad, but mainly in an effort to get away from the few areas that were still on fire.

Clint looked down the street at the hotel that was still burning brighter than ever. Townspeople were doing their best to get everything else away from the inferno, dragging bundles of their possessions wrapped in sections of charred tarp. The flames had left a black trail through the town, winding in between a few tents that were still standing, untouched by the destruction.

"It started there all right," Hank said while pointing as if at a distant storm. "They must've lit up the saloon and the hotel at about the same time and then made a run for it in all the commotion."

"The hotel," Clint said, his words grating painfully in his throat. "What about—?"

Edgar's voice sounded distracted and dead tired. "We ain't got anything to put out a fire like that. We couldn't even do nothing for my place 'cept watch it burn, and we'll have to do the same for the hotel."

"What about your homes?" Clint asked. "What will you do?"

Hank stood to help a passing neighbor who'd stumbled from breathing in too much smoke. "We had fires before. Ain't nothin' so bad as this, but we'll manage. Hell, we saved most of it." Extending a hand, Hank looked down at Clint as though he'd known him his entire life. "Thanks for your help."

Clint took the other man's hand and was helped to his feet. There was still a lot to do before allowing himself to collapse for the night.

FIVE

Three men rode away from Wayne as the small town went up in smoke. The beating of their horses' hooves was lost amid the screams and general panic that always followed a fire, and although they could have been long gone without a trace, the lead rider brought his mount to a stop, turned, and watched the burning spectacle.

Pete Scotelli leaned forward to place one hand on the saddle horn and the other lightly on the back of his horse's neck. He lovingly stroked the animal's mane, eyes locked on to the flames dancing in the distance. "Would ya look at that sight?"

The other two riders came to a stop and waited behind Scotelli. One of them, a nervous-looking kid in his early twenties, seemed ready to break off and start riding away on his own at any moment. The other was a slender man with a week's worth of growth on his face and sharp, bright blue eyes.

"For the love of God, George, does he have to watch every time?" the fidgety kid asked. His anxiousness seemed to infect his horse as well, causing the animal to pace and move about in tight circles.

George Rainer slumped in his saddle as his hand reached for the long rifle that was strapped to the side of his tan gelding. His clothes hung on him like they'd been draped over a scarecrow. His face was clean shaven and smudged from the day's work. A long, deep scar ran lengthwise over his face from the bridge of his nose to his left temple. The top half of his ear on that side had been clipped off as well. "Just give him a minute, you fidgety little bastard. You could use a few breaths yerself."

Trying to keep still was a difficult prospect for Bobby Colville. Just past his twenty-third year, the young man had the mannerisms of a small child and the spirit of an elderly spinster. Both men he was riding with were surprised he hadn't fallen out of his saddle by now. Judging by the look on Rainer's face, he was contemplating giving the young man a push in that direction.

"I just think we should be going while we still can," Colville said in a voice that sounded like a whiny schoolboy. "Someone's bound to see us!"

"Will you shut up before I—"

"He's right," Scotelli interrupted.

Turning in his saddle, Pete Scotelli waved his partner forward, barely acknowledging Bobby's existence. Scotelli was just a little broader in the shoulder than Rainer, yet carried himself with a firm, unquestionable authority. His smooth Italian complexion and fluid motions gave him a slippery appearance that was brought out more when the muscles in his face began to twitch. That twitch was caused by his emotions, either good or bad. When Rainer eased up next to him, Scotelli had a hard time speaking through the spasms in his face. "Someone's coming," he said slowly.

Rainer squinted toward the town and easily plucked out the shape of a man running toward them. The figure was about thirty yards away, waving his hands over his head. He was shouting something, but couldn't be heard over everything else.

The rifle in Rainer's hand was long and slender, resembling an old army model from the war. Only this one took cartridge rounds and had a brass cylinder running from the stock to midway down the barrel. Lifting the rifle and pushing it against his shoulder with one hand, Rainer used his other arm to support and steady the weapon.

He glanced through the scope, straining to find his target. Any other man wouldn't have been able to make out much of anything in the near darkness, but over the years Rainer had proven he was more than most other men the instant he sighted down the length of his custom-made rifle. Breathing deeply, he sat on his horse, steadying the animal with his feet while moving his supporting arm until he drew a bead on the approaching figure.

"I got him, Pete."

"Is he coming this way?" Scotelli asked.

After a short pause, Rainer answered, "Yeah. He sees us."

Hunkering down low in his saddle, Scotelli watched the other man like he was at the theater. He took in the whole sight; the flames, the shadows of people pulling down their own homes in a panic, the cries for help, and now this man stumbling blindly into his own death.

At just the right moment, Scotelli whispered, "Take him."

Rainer's rifle kicked into his shoulder one time as he watched the figure in his scope get knocked onto his back by a high-powered slug.

Scotelli's face twisted into a smile that jumped and shook along with the rest of his twitching face. He saw the vague shape of the man against the backdrop of fire and delighted when it fell at the exact moment that half of the hotel buckled under its own crumbling weight.

"Can we go now?" Colville pleaded.

Scotelli closed his eyes, replaying the final scene in his mind. "Yeah, we can go." Slowly, hesitantly, he turned his horse around and spurred it to a gallop. Colville was close on his heels, but Rainer lingered for a moment to make sure there was nobody else trying to follow them.

Satisfied that there were no more stragglers, the sharpshooter put the rifle back into its harness on his saddle, gave his reins a snap, and followed the other two.

SIX

The only thing left untouched by anything but smoke was the home of Karl Dolffmann. Unlike his hotel, which had burnt to the ground after a little over an hour, Dolffmann's house was far enough away from the blaze to escape being leveled. It stood like a tombstone at the foot of the settlement, marking the smoking pile that had once been Wayne, Nebraska.

The front of the building was blackened and every one of its windows and doors had been flung open to let in the fresh, clean air. A steady flow of townspeople, mostly women and children, were heading for the house. The rest sifted through the mess, saving what they could.

Clint walked next to Edgar through the smoldering plot in the mud that had once been his saloon. The ground was burned dry and felt warm beneath their feet.

"I'm sorry about all this," Clint said earnestly. "I really am."

Edgar stooped down to move a pile of charred wood that used to be the shelves behind his bar. "You didn't set the torch, Mister Adams. You ain't got nothing to be sorry about. 'Sides, you were a help, and we all appreciate what you did."

"Do you think Red had anything to do with this?"

"This town's Red's home, too. He may be mean, but even an animal knows not to shit where it sleeps."

Just then, Hank came walking toward them, instinctually stepping through the general area where the entrance had been.

"Looks like I was right. The biggest fires were here and at the hotel. Damned wind blew hard enough to spread it all around. We're lucky we got to most of the tents before we lost our shelter altogether." Noticing the sorrowful expression on Edgar's face, Hank reached out and put a thick hand on the barkeep's shoulder. "Sorry, Edgar."

Still rooting through the timber, Edgar reached down and pulled a bottle from beneath it all. Although covered with a thick layer of black grime, it was still in one piece. "Looks like it's not a total loss," he said while prying the cork loose.

The barkeep used his shirttail to clean off the rim and took a long pull from the bottle. He passed it to Hank, who downed a healthy swallow, and then handed it over to Clint. The whiskey was sour and hot, but was still the best thing he'd tasted in a long time.

Hank took the bottle and tossed back another swig of the warm liquor. "Most everyone's taken shelter with the German," he said, "but there ain't any rooms left. Luckily the fire didn't get as far as the livery or food sheds, so we'll be able to eat even if we're sleeping outside for a while."

Surveying the damage, Clint watched as people milled about the scorched land and walked toward the end of town. For every tent that was standing, there were three that had been torn down. In a place as small as Wayne, that meant a lot of tearing down. The sight of it was enough to start another kind of fire in the pit of Clint's stomach. "Anything else I can do?" he asked.

"Aww, don't worry 'bout us. We'll have these shelters back up in a day or two."

"That's not what I meant."

Edgar had been thinking quietly as he let the burnt bottle of whiskey rest against his lips. "You can let me finish what I was tryin' to tell you back at the hotel."

"I'm listening."

"About a month or so ago, I got a visit from some fella in a fancy suit. Said he was from Mandrake, Iowa, just outside of Sioux City. He came to my place, and I noticed him right away since he obviously weren't from here. I gave him his drink, and he seemed real neighborly. Askin' how much business I do, how many folks come through town, that sort of thing. Then he asks if I want to sell my saloon."

"He wanted to buy your place?" Clint asked.

"Offered me three hundred dollars, and I won't lie to ya, I was tempted."

Hank was standing over them with his arms folded. Since the last of the fire had died, he seemed about ready to fall down. "That's a helluva lot of money for a tent and a few bottles of 'shine," the big man said.

Nodding, Edgar continued. "That's what I thought, so's I asked him why he would pay so much, and he told me he wanted the land to build a saloon that I could never make on my own. Said it would bring in people with money in their pockets and then more would follow them to build homes and make Wayne somethin' more than a bunch'a tents."

"That's a lot of plans riding on one saloon," Clint said.

"Well, he was pretty convincing, until I decided to keep my place and run it my own way."

Edgar watched his feet as he ground his toe into the dirt and ash. "Then he got real serious. Told me to take the money while I could because he'd have the land either way."

"And what did you do?"

Laughing, Edgar looked straight at Clint and raised his bottle in the air for a halfhearted toast. "I had some of the local boys toss him on his prissy ass and told him if he wanted to drink, he'd have to stick his face in a creek."

Clint and Hank couldn't help but laugh at the thought of Edgar laying down the law. They all laughed long enough to release some of the tension that had been building inside of them. When it died down, Edgar sounded forlorn and regretful.

"Before he left, he said his associates would be back to burn my place down around my ears. Said it would be my fault if the entire town came down as well."

"This wasn't your fault, Edgar," Clint said. "By the looks of things, I'd say the owner of the hotel refused to sell out, also. You say this man came from outside of Sioux City?"

"Mandrake, Iowa. He had a card with his address on it. Name was Ken Styles."

"Do you have the card?"

"Sure. I kept it right over there," Edgar said while pointing to a pile of smoldering ash.

Clint stood and dusted himself off. "Do you know of anyone else who talked to a man like this?"

Edgar shook his head. "Can't rightly say, but when he took off, he was headed toward the hotel. Could've just been looking for a room."

"I doubt it," Clint said.

Suddenly, there was the sound of running footsteps heading down the middle of the street.

"Someone! Anyone!" a youthful voice shouted. "My pa's been shot!"

Clint, Hank, and Edgar sprung to their feet and found a twelve-year-old girl at the middle of a growing throng of people. The girl's face was smudged with black just the same as everyone else's and clear streaks marked where tears were streaming down her cheeks.

"Who's been shot?" Hank asked.

"My pa!"

Clint looked to where the girl was pointing to see another smaller group huddled around the figure of a man stretched out behind one of the few remaining tents. Edgar, who'd already run over to the body and back, arrived at Clint's side, breathing heavily from the burst of activity.

"He's dead all right. Ol' Harvey Withers. Someone shot him plum in the chest."

Clint led a group of townspeople to search the area, but found nothing in the darkness. He didn't need to see any more to know what he had to do. Walking back toward the livery as the group dispersed for the night, he passed Edgar, who watched as the little girl and her mother were led to the German's house at the edge of town.

"I'd better find a place to get some rest," Clint said as the flames inside him were fanned even higher. "It looks like I'll be heading out to Iowa tomorrow morning."

SEVEN

Clint spent the night in the stables. He wasn't the only one there and the large bales of hay gave comfort to twice as many people as horses that evening. The animals had been tied up outside while two of the townspeople took turns on a rotating watch to make sure nothing happened to the stock. The funny thing was that the inside of the horses' stalls was the freshest smelling place in the entire town.

Although the scent of hay and closely packed bodies was no spring rain, it sure beat the hot smoke that still drifted down the street after the fire. Clint found a corner that was unoccupied, pulled his hat down over his eyes, and drifted quickly off to sleep. He thought it would be harder to get himself to relax, but the frantic pace of the last few hours was more than enough to knock him out.

When he awoke, the stables were already empty.

The entire town of Wayne was busy picking itself up, dusting itself off, and starting over again. Men were driving posts into the ground to rebuild frames that would hold the canvas, which the women were busy stitching. Even the children were earning their keep by wandering the area and picking up all the debris and separating it according to usefulness.

Clint walked over to where the horses were tied and quickly found Eclipse standing next to a white mare.

"No time for that, boy," Clint said as he led the stallion

away toward a pile of saddles. Finding his own, he fixed it onto the horse's back and prepared himself for the day's ride. As he was checking his bags, Clint heard someone approaching from behind.

It was Edgar. "We'll be fine, you know," the barkeep said.

Clint turned to find the other man standing in a fresh set of clothes that looked about two sizes too big for his bony frame. "I can tell. Has your town been through something like this before?"

"We had fires, but nothing so big. We seen a twister, though. Came through these parts a few years back and pulled up all our crops and took off with some of the animals as well. That was back when we were closer to the river."

"Why move so far away?"

"Floods."

Clint shook his head. "You've got a tough little town here. A bit unlucky perhaps, but still awful tough."

Reaching up to stroke Eclipse's mane, Edgar turned his face away as if trying not to meet Clint's gaze. "We'll make it through just fine, but we sure could use another hand around here."

"I've got an appointment to keep in Mandrake."

"That ain't necessary," Edgar said. "They had their way and burned us down. What more could they do?"

"You'd be surprised." Looking over the town and all those working to put it back together, Clint only wished he could get his hands on whoever had set that fire when they were still here. "Whoever came to you before wasn't just looking for someplace to burn, Edgar. My guess is they didn't even want your saloon. They wanted your land. All this was just to clear it off."

Clint swung himself up into the saddle and let Eclipse fuss for a bit.

"But what's so special about this place?" Edgar asked. "We ain't nothin' but a camp. Hell, a stiff breeze could knock down everything here 'cept for the hotel and the German's house. You think he had somethin' to do with this?"

"I doubt anyone would set fire to a prosperous business just to make a point. There's something else going on, and I doubt its going to stop here. I can't let the people responsible for this go on and burn up other people's homes and businesses. I'll bet Wayne isn't even the first town to see this happen."

"So who'd want this land so bad they'd be willin' to kill for it?"

Clint had been thinking so much about the fire that he'd nearly forgot about the man who'd been shot. Remembering the death only made him want to ride out faster. "I don't know yet, but that's why I'm going to Mandrake."

Reining Eclipse so that he was headed northeast, Clint worked out the ride in his head. He'd heard of the town of Mandrake, Iowa, but had only passed through it once. It was bigger than average, but nothing special. Nice saloon with a few honest poker dealers.

"Could I ask you a favor?" Edgar said.

Clint looked down while pulling back on the reins. Sensing the ride ahead, Eclipse was already anxious to get going.

Edgar looked back at him with a strength in his eyes that seemed to have grown there since the flames took his home. "Can I ask you to come back through town when you've done what you're set to do? Even if you just find out what's going on and decide to move on? At least let us know what happened. It'll help us sleep better."

"Don't worry, Edgar. I'll be back. That 'shine of yours does wonders for my sinuses. Hopefully, I'll have good news for you when I sit down in your new place for another drink."

With that, Clint pointed Eclipse in the right direction and let the stallion take off at full speed.

EIGHT

The Platte River crept along behind the cabin so slowly that it didn't even have the energy to make much noise. Most rivers sounded alike: running water, trickling falls, maybe some fish splashing about. But this one just laid there like a lazy, dirty old man. Not even deep enough at this bend to drown a grass-hopper, the Platte was nothing more than a giant puddle in Pete Scotelli's backyard.

His cabin was built from logs solid enough to withstand the yearly flooding, but not put together well enough to keep the light out. Stray beams slipped between the cracks and got into the eyes of a slender man sitting at a table in the middle of the cabin's single room. He was busy dabbing at a mud stain on his pant leg using a white cotton handkerchief.

"Where are the rest of your. . . . compatriots?" Ken Styles asked.

Scotelli stood opposite the door, flipping a small pocketknife between his fingers. "I only got one partner. Your boss stuck me with that pansy-assed kid."

"Yes, well, they felt the need to keep track of you, and Bobby is good at that if nothing else. Where are they?"

"Fetching supplies. You got my money?"

Finished with the mud stain, Styles began brushing dust from his lapels. "Someone from the bank in Omaha will ride down with the money as soon as I return."

"Too scared to bring it yerself?"

"No, my hesitation is purely practical. I've dealt with enough of your kind to know better than to do business without taking certain precautions."

"Then why are you out here? Is it the fresh air or just to sit in my home and flick your dirt on my floor?"

Styles held his hand still just as he was about to brush another dusty patch off his suit. Slowly, he folded the handkerchief and fitted it precisely into place in his breast pocket. "I'm here to tell you about the payment arrangement and to offer you another job."

Scotelli's eyes lit up. "Another job? Who do you want handled this time?"

"Maybe nobody. I'll be riding up north toward the Nebraska and South Dakota border. Depending on how my negotiations go, I may not need you for anything more than to escort me on my journey. On the other hand, things may get . . . messy."

"Just like before?"

"Yes, Mister Scotelli. Just like before."

Styles had made a healthy living being able to read other people. None of those skills were necessary, however, to read the man in front of him. The excited twitch in Scotelli's face told it all. Rising to his feet as though he was about to excuse himself from a banquet table, Styles bent to retrieve a leather case that had been sitting at his feet and walked across the room.

"You do remember that this is all strictly business?" Styles asked.

"What the hell is that supposed to mean?"

The man in the suit stepped closer to the door and had it open before he replied. "It means I don't want to see any more of what happened in Wayne. The job was to take out the saloon and the hotel. Shooting bystanders wasn't in the contract."

Scotelli crossed his arms and walked over to the businessman. "George has his job, too," he said when he was standing toe to toe with the smaller gentleman, "which is to make sure there ain't no witnesses."

"Be that as it may, our employer doesn't like unnecessary blood on his hands. Keep your dogs at bay, Mister Scotelli, and try to make sure that any bodies that turn up on the next job are burnt in the fire."

"Or what?" Scotelli asked in a voice that cut like a finely honed blade.

Surprisingly enough, Styles didn't back down. "Or there won't be a next job."

Both men stared at each other for a few seconds that dragged by like hours. Finally, Scotelli nodded. "Fair enough," he said.

Styles turned crisply on his heels and walked out the door to a horse and buggy waiting outside. After he'd climbed into the driver's seat, he noticed George Rainer standing with his rifle ready next to the cabin.

"Oh, and Kenny," Scotelli shouted. "Make sure that man from the bank gets here quick or maybe someone'll have to dig your body out from underneath a pile of ashes."

Without responding to the threat, Styles gave his reins a snap and sent his buggy down the ruts leading away from the Platte.

Omaha, Nebraska, had been one of the last civilized stops the pioneers had seen before their westward trek across the plains. In the days when the wagon trains took so many families into their new lives in the frontier, Omaha would be the final reminder of the life they'd left behind. And for all those people passing through, there were always some who decided not to leave.

That accounted for the outskirts of the town being composed mainly of tents and temporary structures similar to those that made up the entire town of Wayne. Unlike that town, Omaha had real buildings in its core and plenty of people walking streets that were becoming more populated by the week.

The Third Bank of Omaha wasn't the biggest in town, but it was definitely one of the most prosperous. Not that anyone could figure that out by appearances. The small building on the edge of a small business district looked less impressive than some of the gambling dens. It was ignored by folk who were more impressed with the bigger banks, which was precisely what the owners wanted. It was built right next to the sheriff's office, which had taken no small amount of dealing in itself.

The end result was a fat, yet forgotten vault sitting in a place that put it under the protection of the sheriff himself. There was no deal worked out between the Third Bank of Omaha and the law, but there didn't need to be. It was so close to the sheriff's desk that robbing it would be more trouble than it was worth.

At least, that was what most people would think.

Others knew better. Namely the man who rode his buggy up to the bank and hopped down to the street. Although men as well dressed as Ken Styles were not a common sight in Omaha, most of the people on the streets had seen him before. Him as well as some of the other dandies that took their business to that particular bank.

Styles returned a casual wave from the sheriff, who was sitting outside his office, before opening the door to the bank and stepping inside. The front area was just big enough to make it uncomfortable for more than three people to be in there at once. There was only one window, which was always covered with a sign that read "Be Back Later." Most folks found this lack of service annoying enough for them to take their business elsewhere. Styles ignored the sign and walked straight through the door marked EMPLOYEES.

There was an office behind the teller window that made most closets look roomy in comparison. Sitting at a small, broken-down desk was an elderly man in shirtsleeves and a visor.

"Mister Jenkins," Styles said to the old man, "please deliver Mister Scotelli's payment right away."

"I'll get to it after lunch, sir."

"No. You'd better get to it now. And have a telegram sent to our people in Mandrake letting them know that the next job should be right on schedule and casualties should be down from the last one. Also tell them that the property in Wayne should be ready for acquisition. Did anything come for me?"

"Yes, sir," the old man said while pointing to a basket on top of the desk.

Picking up the only paper inside the basket, Styles looked

over the telegram and nodded slowly. The message was short and straightforward, just like Styles himself.

"Did you read this?" Styles asked.

The old man started to shake his head no, but stopped and shrugged. "Couldn't help it, sir."

Styles reached into his pocket and fished out a cigar and a metal case with his initials engraved on one side and the picture of a woman's silhouette on another. He opened it with a flick of his thumb, removed a match, and struck it on a rough surface along one of the container's edges. After lighting his cigar and taking a few puffs, Styles topped off his ritual by dropping the match safe back into his inside jacket pocket.

"Well, try to forget what you read, Jenkins. If Scotelli or any of his men know about that telegram, they'll kill the messenger first and then me."

Still holding the lit match in one hand, Styles touched the flame to the corner of the telegram. The paper curled at the edges and quickly became more dust on the floor.

NINE

The ride to Mandrake was a short and uneventful one.

Partly due to Eclipse's eagerness to run and partly due to the featureless expanse that was most of Iowa, Clint found himself coming up on to the town in record time. It had grown a lot since the last time he'd been there. Where before it had been mostly a few houses and a short stretch of small businesses, Mandrake was now a booming community alive with commerce and not one, but two main streets.

At first, Clint thought he'd come to the wrong place. Even the outskirts of Mandrake had changed beyond his recognition. There were rows of small houses and a blacksmith's shop situated along the banks of a small creek, which powered a fair-sized mill. Beyond those houses was a general store and carpenter. Beyond that was the Mandrake Inn and a restaurant that was teeming with the dinner crowd by the time Clint rode past it.

People seemed friendly enough as they all went about their way. At the end of Second Street was a building marked as the sheriff's office. Clint made a mental note of that and headed to the next street over so he could get a quick feel for the rest of the town.

Third Street was one of the busiest in town. The sun was nearly gone, bringing out the sounds of raucous laughter and raised voices from a row of gambling parlors on one side of the street. A row of opium dens and bordellos lined the other. At the head of it all was a large, two-story building where all the rest of the people on the street appeared to either be coming from or heading toward. Stretching across its entire front was a sign written in bold, red letters that read PRAIRIE DOG SALOON.

More than once, Clint had to make sharp turns to keep Eclipse from trampling a drunk or two who seemed too oblivious to realize where they were walking. Heading away from the Prairie Dog, he came to an intersection where the nightlife met the rest of the world and bawdy houses gave way to laundries and storefronts.

He got directions to the livery from a man returning home from a hard day's work.

"There's three in town," the man told him, "but the best one's at the end of Main Street. All the others are full now anyway."

Clint thanked him and moved on.

The farther he went, the busier the town became. Last time he'd been here, Mandrake was a sleepy little place where a handful of farmers had staked their claim and raised their families. Now, the place was so busy, it made him wonder where the prosperity was coming from.

There was a railroad stop nearby, but nothing that would bring in this many people. He'd spotted a farm and a few cattle ranches on the way in, but nothing big enough to attract much attention. Hell, if he hadn't been there once before, Clint would never have even heard of Mandrake, but here it was; a town nearly big enough to give Dodge City a run for its money.

Main Street was easy enough to find. As soon as the noise from Third began to fade, Clint could hear another set of voices howling at the setting sun. It was hard to tell which street was louder since at some point between them, the ruckus from one end of town mixed in with the commotion from the other. Instinctively, Clint tried to skirt the excitement since Eclipse seemed to finally be tiring out.

The stallion's ears twitched at all the shouting as they got closer to it, and his hooves scraped irritably at the ground with most of his steps.

"I know how you feel, boy," Clint said to the horse. "I could do with some peace and quiet myself."

Eclipse was a long ways off from panicking or rearing from the ruckus and occasional gunshots. Still, both horse and rider had had a long day, and when they reached the livery at the end of Main Street, Eclipse let out a contented sigh.

The man running the livery had a long black beard and looked only slightly smaller than some of the stock in his barn. He was half asleep in a rickety chair, with his feet propped up on a bale of hay. Even when a pair of rowdy men across the street began wailing "Camptown Races" at the top of their lungs, the liveryman barely seemed to notice.

"Excuse me," Clint said as he hopped to the ground.

Only then did the large liveryman move a muscle: fat cheeks puffing like a fish's when he let out a rumbling belch and brought a hand up to cover his mouth. " 'Scuse me, is more like it. What can I do for ya?"

"I need to put my horse up for a while," Clint said. "I could also use a hotel. Is there any place quiet enough around here where I can get some sleep?"

The liveryman paused while he seemed to think the question over. Instead of an answer, another burp came from behind his bushy beard. Finally, he said, "There's boardinghouses over along First Street. Some on Copper as well. How long you stayin'?"

"Not sure."

"Then you can check in with me before you leave so's we can discuss payment. Nice horse," he said while taking hold of Eclipse's reins. "Darley?"

"Darley Arabian," Clint corrected. "How long has the town been like this?"

"I've lived here my whole life and this ain't been nothin but your average place to live. Can't stand city life, so I stayed here and took over my pa's business. Wouldn't you know it, but about a year or two back, it goes from the Mandrake I knew to what you see here. Damn shame. If it weren't for there bein' nobody to take over my place, I'd pack up and head out."

"All this sprung up in two years?"

"Sure enough. Made a lot of folks rich in the process, too.

Mainly them's that own the saloons. They're the worst. They'd have ya killed if'n they thought there was any money in it."

That last statement caught Clint's attention. His eyes snapped away from his horse to the man tending to him. "What do you mean by that?"

"Town like this, with two saloons angling for all the money, makes business between 'em all pretty cutthroat. Sheriff's gotten a lot of headaches trying to keep them two away from each other."

"Which two?"

"Owners of the two biggest places in town. The Three Aces and the Prairie Dog. They fight like they was family."

Clint wanted to ask some more questions, but didn't want to make his own business in Mandrake common knowledge. Instead, he held his tongue and removed his saddlebags.

"You stay in the Prairie Dog, you tell the owner I sent ya. Name's Arlen."

"I don't suppose you'd put your percentage from that recommendation toward my livery fees?"

Arlen scrunched his face up and his beard twisted into a wide grin. "Dammit if this town don't make connivers outta us all. Tell ya what. You mention my name and stay at the Prairie Dog, and I'll knock off ten percent."

"Good enough," Clint said. "You sound like you know an awful lot for someone who tries to keep his nose out of things."

"Man's gotta eat. Plus bein' around all this gambling doesn't help one much."

Tossing his bags over his shoulder, Clint walked out of the livery and headed back toward the Prairie Dog. After all, ten percent was ten percent.

TEN

Third Street seemed even rowdier when Clint wasn't looking down at it from the top of his horse. Those groups of drunks were now enough to run him over instead of the other way around. And since the sun had set, there seemed to be a whole lot more of them staggering down the street.

At the center of all the commotion was the Prairie Dog Saloon. On the outside, it was a weather-beaten reminder of what the town had once been. It looked like it had to have been one of the first buildings in Mandrake, with its warped wooden planks and peeling layers of paint. When he got closer to it, Clint thought he might have stopped in here on his last visit.

Straining his memory, Clint realized he had been inside the Prairie Dog, but only for a beer and a few hands of five card draw. That was when the saloon had been the only one in town, marking Mandrake's eastern limit.

A lot had changed since then.

Although the Prairie Dog still looked run down, there were spots of fresh paint along the second level and the steps leading up from the street seemed fairly new. Also, the building itself had been expanded to more than double its former size. It wasn't hard to believe the owner would have enough to pay for renovations since the place was busting at the rafters with people in all stages of drunkenness and engaging in every form of sin.

Clint walked through a set of double doors, stepping aside to let a gambler and his female prize for the night walk out and head for her room across the street. Bigger than two barns, the Prairie Dog Saloon was half bar and half stage. It was similar to many others Clint had seen, but what it lacked in originality it made up for in pure size. The bar ran no less than fifty feet and still didn't make it to the other side of the room. Four men in white aprons poured drinks and chewed the fat with at least thirty drinkers.

On the opposite side of the room was a stage with a dozen showgirls. All of them were spinning on high heels to the songs being played by a man at a piano that was only a quarter-note out of tune. Four roulette wheels spun while gamblers wandered between them and tables where everything from poker to faro were being dealt by men in crisp white shirts and green armbands.

It was too crowded for Clint to see how many gaming tables there were, but the number was up well past twenty. What struck him most was the sheer wildness of the crowd. He half expected to see men swinging from the garish chandeliers hanging overhead.

The place should have been a lawman's nightmare. Clint had been around enough saloons to know that having so many men together while drinking and gambling was a dangerous thing. Still, although the place was definitely rowdy, and there was the occasional fist thrown here and there, he could see no real fights in the works or even the evidence of past ones. No broken tables or chairs. No shattered glasses. Even the mirror behind the bar was clean and in good condition.

It seemed the good people of Mandrake took pride in their saloons.

Even so, Clint was tempted to turn around and find a nice quiet boardinghouse far away from all the commotion. Then again, he figured he'd have to sleep on the ground miles away from town if he wanted to have anything close to perfect quiet. There was also something about what the liveryman had said that made Clint want to be closer to the inner workings of the town. And if anything was happening in Mandrake, it seemed it would be happening in one of its saloons.

Clint moved away from the door and walked toward the end of the bar. Almost immediately he was greeted by one of the four bartenders. The man, like the other three, wore a white apron and looked to be in his early thirties. His thinning hair had been slicked back to match a waxed mustache that was curled up at either end. A pug nose supported a pair of wire-framed spectacles and his hands worked busily at drying off a large glass mug.

"What can I get for ya?" the bartender asked.

"Why don't I start with a room for the night?"

"Just a room, or would you like a pretty little someone to go with it?"

Looking around the bar, Clint noticed several working girls had already begun circling him. While they looked attractive enough, he waved away the offer. "A room will do for the moment. Arlen told me you had some of the best."

"See the lady at the counter down past the bar. She's got the keys. Come on down once you're settled and see why we're the best entertainment in this or any town you've been to."

Clint felt a hand snaking around his waist and another across his chest. Then the smell of jasmine drifted into the air. Turning, he found a voluptuous brunette in a low-cut dress reaching around to lock her arms around him. "Or you don't have to leave your room at all," she said. "I can bring up your dinner and then you can have dessert until the sun comes up."

But Clint had already eased out of the brunette's embrace and was making his way through the milling crowd. Before he was halfway down the length of the bar, the working girls had descended upon their newest targets.

He hadn't seen the counter when he'd first walked in. He still couldn't see it until he was nearly at the end of the bar where the crowd began to thin out. It looked like a smaller version of a hotel check-in desk, complete with bell and register. Clint tapped the bell, but couldn't even hear the sound it made over all the background noise.

Apparently someone had heard it and soon a narrow door behind the counter opened to allow a woman to walk through, who instantly struck Clint as the prettiest thing he'd seen since riding into town.

She stood a full head shorter than him in a low-cut red dress that showed off an impressive hourglass figure. She wore thin strands of silver around her neck, which blended perfectly with her cool, pale skin. Her eyes were soft brown, and she had a single streak of white running through thick, coal-black hair that flowed over her shoulders. She walked with a spring in her step that set every part of her into motion.

"Do you want me?" she asked playfully.

"Well, who wouldn't?"

"You rang the bell, handsome, so what can I do for you?"

Clint adjusted the bags on his shoulder and leaned forward to hear her better. She smelled of wine and spicy perfume. "I need a room. Arlen told me this would be the best place to stay in town."

"Looks like you're new to Mandrake," she said while pointing toward his saddlebags. "Here for business or pleasure?"

"Most of one and some of the other. Right now, I'm looking forward to getting off my feet and then something to eat."

The woman gave Clint a long look and turned the register around for him. Handing him a pen, she placed her elbows on the counter and leaned forward as he signed in, giving Clint a generous view of her large, sloping breasts.

"My name is Madeline Lowell. Damn near everyone calls me Maddy. So which is it Mister—" Leaning forward even more, she craned her neck to see what he'd written. "—Adams?"

"Which is what?"

"Mostly business or mostly pleasure?"

"I haven't quite decided yet."

Maddy snatched a key from a board nailed inside the narrow doorway, closed the door, and walked around the desk. "I'll take you to your room and maybe you'll have your mind made up before I get a meal in your belly."

As he followed her to a staircase in the far corner of the saloon, Clint watched her generous hips swaying beneath her dress. The way she looked at him over her shoulder, she knew he was looking. After that the spring in her step increased and her hips danced even more beneath the folds of her dress.

Once they reached the second floor, she went to room number eight, unlocked it and went inside. The first thing Clint noticed when he went through the door was the large, four-poster bed taking up most of the space. Maddy had her back to him with her arms stretched out to touch either post at the foot of the bed. Her dress hung open at her back and was sliding slowly down her body.

"Close the door," she whispered.

ELEVEN

Clint stepped inside his room and dropped his bags to the floor. "I hope this isn't the same welcome that everyone gets when they come in off the street," he said.

Turning around, Maddy let the top of her dress come down just a little more. Her skin was smooth and creamy. The fabric of her clothing had dropped just low enough to show a glimpse of small, dark brown nipples. "Not everyone. Just the ones that I like." Moving forward, she shrugged her shoulders, allowing the dress to drop to her waist. A firm, rounded stomach was the only thing keeping it up.

Maddy reached out to unbutton Clint's shirt. "And I'll be honest with you. I don't like a lot of the trash that comes through here. But the ones I do like"—now she was working at the buckle of his pants. Before sliding them off, she felt along Clint's thighs and cupped the swollen package between his legs—"they never complained once about entertaining the hostess for a change."

Clint allowed himself to be undressed as his hands started exploring the full curves of Maddy's figure. "So you're the hostess?" he asked.

"Among other things."

"Aren't you taking away some of the business from your girls downstairs?"

"They had their chance," she purred while stepping out of

the dress that had fallen into a bundle around her ankles. "Besides, it'd be a shame to make you pay for something that any one of them would gladly do for free if they were in my boots."

Clint was bare chested and savoring the feel of Maddy's capable hands easing his pants down over his hips. "But they're not in your boots."

"No, they're not, but I am." And those boots were all she was wearing. Pivoting on her toes, Maddy strutted toward the bed, showcasing a set of curves that would inspire most painters. Her backside was wide and full, quivering only slightly with every step. Her velvety boots were laced all the way up to her knees, hugging her calves as she crawled onto the bed.

Clint eagerly finished undressing, his penis aching to feel Maddy's milky skin rubbing against his own. She was on all fours facing away from him, her hands stretched out to grip on to the headboard. Clint hung his gun belt on the headboard, within easy reach, and joined her on the bed. When she felt his weight drop onto the mattress, she dropped down onto her elbows and raised her plump buttocks into the air.

That was all the invitation Clint needed since he felt he was going to explode if he didn't enter her soon. Gripping her hips in his hands, he pulled her toward him and impaled her with his cock. She felt warm and moist and when he slid all the way inside of her, she squeezed her legs together and began laughing deep in the back of her throat.

"That's it, handsome," she moaned. "Now do it hard. I like it hard, baby."

Hearing her voice only made Clint want her more, and he obliged her request by driving into her until his body was slapping loudly against her rump.

As soon as his pace quickened, Maddy relaxed her legs and started crawling forward. She was giggling mischievously when she pulled herself close to the headboard and disengaged herself from Clint's body. The break in contact was brief, but enough for him to regain some of his senses. Hearing her girlish laughter, Clint slapped Maddy on her backside just hard enough to make her squeal.

"Oh!" she yelped as she flipped around to face him. The lustful smile on her face only widened when she reached back to rub her behind. "That's what I like. But I'm still the boss around here. Now it's my turn." She ran her nails gently between his legs and stroked his shaft up and down. Then her touch wandered over his stomach until her palm was on his chest, and she was shoving him over.

"Lean back," she commanded.

Clint did as he was told and felt her warm body settling onto his. Her hand guided his rigid member until it was once again between her legs. She impaled herself on his rod and eased all of her weight down until he couldn't push any farther into her. Then her hips began moving in tiny circles and gently bucking back and forth.

Once again, he was brought to the brink only to be eased away from it when she climbed off of him. When Clint opened his eyes, he saw Maddy standing on the bed, looking down at him with her hands on her hips. Those black velvet boots stepped forward until there was one on either side of his head.

"Since you're my special guest," she said as she bent at the knees, "you get your dessert first." And then she lowered her sex down onto Clint's mouth. The lips between her thighs were hot and moist.

At first, Clint was a little surprised by the woman's straightforwardness, but once he felt her juices run down his face, he was reaching up with both hands to grab hold of that rounded butt and pulling her in closer. He couldn't hear much with her legs pressed against his ears, but he could still make out the sound of her screaming with ecstasy as his tongue went to work inside of her.

Her cries reached their peak and her legs locked tightly around his head. Her hands reached down to grab him by the hair until finally he could feel the strength drain out of her. She raised herself off of him and looked down, her hair falling like a black waterfall over her shoulders.

"Now don't you think for one moment that I'm skipping my dessert," she said while standing on the mattress and turning to face the other direction.

She dropped back down on top of him and the thin, pink lips between her legs were once again kissing him on the mouth. This time, however, her body was draped over his chest and stomach, allowing her to lick her own juices from his shaft.

Her mouth took in Clint's pole and sucked on it like it was a stick of candy. He could feel her hair tickling his thighs as her head bobbed up and down. She noisily devoured him while he ran his hands along the curve of her hips. When he started to moan, she kept on working. And when he exploded inside her mouth, she sucked him until he was dry.

Maddy swung her leg around and knelt on the bed facing him. The tip of her tongue came out to lick the corner of her ruby-painted lips. "Welcome to the Prairie Dog," she said.

Madeline Lowell was just as comfortable out of her clothes as she was when in them. She moved around Clint's room wearing nothing but those high velvet boots while straightening the bed as well as every little piece of wrinkled fabric from the tablecloth to the throw rug. When she stood in front of the open window to adjust the curtains, she arched her back and savored the feel of the night breeze against her skin.

Clint moved around behind her and placed his hands on her hips. He then ran his fingers up to brush against her full breasts, feeling the nipples grow harder in the cool air.

"Was all this because I mentioned Arlen's name?" he asked.

"If I didn't like the looks of you so much, I'd have had you tossed out for mentioning that horse's ass." Turning to face him, Maddy ignored the catcalls from someone down on the street who'd happened to look up at Clint's window. "You must be hungry."

"I did manage to work up an appetite."

"Then give me a few minutes to check in with my workers and meet me in the dining room." She slid her hand down between his legs and ran her nails along his cock, causing it to twitch and stir. Strutting over to her dress, she made a show of bending down to pick it up. Maddy slipped into her clothes and was heading for the door before Clint had his shirt tucked in.

After she'd left, Clint sat on the edge of his bed and looked around. He hadn't had much of a chance to get a good look at his room before and now that he was alone, he had time to be impressed with his surroundings.

The room was spacious and had all the trimmings. Besides the large comfortable bed, there was also a good-sized dresser and a table with washbasin and towel. Expensive looking curtains framed a single window looking down on the bustling activity of Third Street. There was even a dark red area rug covering a floor made of polished wood.

Suddenly, Clint wondered how a place like this could have been running without him even hearing about it. In the circle of card players he knew, he heard about most of the great saloons, and still the Prairie Dog went unmentioned. Could this have been so new that word hadn't had a chance to circulate? And what about the other place in town on Main Street? Arlen had mentioned something about fierce competition between them.

Clint couldn't help but wonder if Mandrake's other saloon could even compare with this one. On the other hand, if it boasted half the comforts Clint had already experienced at the Prairie Dog, he was more than happy to give it a try.

What grounded his thoughts was a mental reminder of why he was there to begin with. The man responsible for burning down a small town of poor farmers was somehow connected to the business being run in Mandrake. According to Edgar, the only people approached before the torch was set were hotel and saloon owners.

Now, Clint was thinking about all the questions he wanted to ask the Prairie Dog's hostess over dinner. Hopefully, she would let him talk a bit more when they were out in the open. Then again, from what he'd seen of Maddy, being in a public place might not do much to keep her in line.

TWELVE

The cabin on the washed out bank of the Platte stood by itself amid a group of dead trees. A layer of orange and brown leaves had just begun to cover the ground, some drifting out to float on the still waters. These waters didn't run deep, however, as shown by the pair of men who walked across the river without having to wade in past the tops of their boots.

George Rainer sloshed through the cold water like he was crossing the street, while Bobby Colville followed timidly behind. The younger kid looked fearful of ruining a suit that had already been dirtied beyond repair after the ride to and from Wayne. The door to the cabin opened slightly, and even from the river, the barrel of a pistol could be seen poking beyond the frame.

By the time Rainer had made it to dry land, the cabin door had swung wide open to let Pete Scotelli step outside.

"Find anything out there?" Scotelli asked while holstering his 45.

Rainer scraped his heels along the ground, trying to kick the mud from the bottom of his feet. "Just some old man on a worn-out mule heading up the road. Didn't seem to be in much of a hurry."

"That'd be Orville Jenkins riding in from Omaha. He's bringing us our pay for the job we finished."

It was at this time that Colville staggered from the water,

nearly slipping on a patch of mossy rocks. "I need to get my horse," he said in exasperation.

Scotelli's face darkened when he looked at the pudgy kid. "What the hell are you talking about?"

"I need a horse so I can head back into town and check the telegraph office. I sent word to my employer, and I was supposed to get a reply soon after."

"You want a horse? You can see about hitching a ride with Orville after he pays us. I bet you two'd get along just fine."

Rainer's laugh was more of a disgusted grunt. "This kid whines like an old woman, so he might as well ride with someone who's used to it."

Although the kid seemed perturbed by the other men's ridicule, Colville didn't have the sand to say much of anything about it. Instead, he shifted angrily on his feet and balled his hands into little fists.

"Take it easy, Bobby," Scotelli said as if he was trying to calm a fussy child. "We'd hate to do anything to make us look bad in that report of yours."

Colville straightened up. "You certainly wouldn't. Otherwise, you might not—"

"Might not what?" Rainer growled as he stepped up to stare directly into Colville's face.

The kid swallowed nervously and pulled at the edges of his suit jacket. "You might not get as many well paying jobs if your behavior doesn't improve."

"You hear that, George?" Scotelli asked with a dramatic shudder. "We better shape up or the old lady here is gonna cry to her old man."

Both men started laughing wholeheartedly and didn't stop until Orville's mule could be heard clomping toward the cabin. Bobby Colville tried to maintain his dignity by storming away from the pair to go and meet the mule and its rider.

Orville looked as though the ride from Omaha had been enough to rattle his bones out of their sockets. When he climbed down from the saddle, it was all he could do to keep from falling flat on his back after his legs proved almost too shaky to support his weight. He was plenty used to riding; it wasn't the trail or the animal that had worn him out. It was the heavy bags lying over his shoulders that made his back hurt and his knees buckle.

In all his years of working as the courier and teller for the Third Bank of Omaha, he'd never made a delivery without having the money on his person at all times. He'd seen enough in his years to know better than to leave anything of value out in the open. These days, however, his aching bones were begging for a change in that little policy.

Fortunately, Colville knew to be there to keep Orville upright when he climbed down off his tired old mule. "Let me take that for you," he said as he reached for the bags.

In his earlier years, Orville would have refused such an offer. Now, he thanked the stars for it. "I'd be much obliged if you'd hand that over to Mister Scotelli."

Grudgingly, Colville took the bags and placed them in Scotelli's waiting hands. The Italian hefted the weight in his hands before opening the flap and looking inside. "Keep them both here," he said to Rainer. "I'm going to count this up, and if we're square, they can both get the hell outta my sight."

After Scotelli disappeared inside the cabin and slammed the door, Rainer leaned against a tree with his hand resting on the butt of his pistol. With the burden removed from their backs, both Orville and his mule seemed to be perking up. The old man started pacing back and forth while swinging his arms at his sides.

"Gets the circulation going," he said by way of explanation. Looking over to Colville, the old man dropped his voice so only the kid could hear him. "So, everything still moving along with those friends of yours?"

Colville turned his back to Rainer before answering. "They're hardly friends and nothing went as smoothly as we'd thought."

"I hear you ran into some trouble. Mister Styles told me there was a man shot."

"That's right," Colville said a little too loudly. "I saw it."

The old timer nodded slowly without much emotion. "Well, that happens sometimes. I hear you'll be heading home soon anyways."

"Really?" Colville said with a gleam in his eye.

"Yeah," Rainer said from behind them. "Really?"

Turning at the same time, Colville and the old man saw that Rainer had crept up so that he had managed to close most of the distance between them without anyone being the wiser. He hadn't drawn his gun, but Rainer was tensed and ready for action if the need should arise.

"I thought the old woman there was supposed to stick with us so's he could make his reports," Rainer said.

Orville felt a cold panic slipping through his stomach, but did his best not to let on. "Was he supposed to stay? What do I know? I guess I heard wrong."

Just then, the door to the cabin burst open and Orville's bags came flying outside to land heavily at Colville's feet. They were full enough to make a loud thump when they hit, which frightened the slope-backed mule. Instinctively, Orville reached out for the pack animal. At first, he wanted to calm the mule down. When he looked around to see what had been thrown his way and caught the look on Scotelli's face, he needed to use the shifting animal for support.

Scotelli stormed down the path leading from the door to the river bank and stood glaring angry daggers into Orville's eyes. "Where's the rest of it, old man?" he growled.

Having already sized up the situation, Rainer pulled his own pistol out to cover his partner's move.

"What . . . what do you mean?" Orville stammered. "The rest of what?"

"Our money you dusty son of a bitch! That's not even half of what I was promised!"

Now Colville stepped between Scotelli and the old man. "There's just got to be a mistake here." He was about to try his hand at negotiations when he saw Rainer pointing a gun in his direction. "Now, just a minute. . . ."

"That why you were fixin' to leave so soon?" Rainer asked.

Scotelli's head snapped around to look at his partner. "What?"

"I heard them two talkin'. The old man said little Colville was set to go home soon."

Looking from the kid to Orville to the bag and back again, Scotelli's face broke into a sly grimace. He pointed his gun at Orville and cocked it. "Why don't you start talking to me, instead."

"I . . . I don't know what to say."

"Well, I don't like the way this is adding up, so you'd better think of something to make me feel better."

"I . . . there was . . . I think . . . you can't . . ."

Glancing over to Rainer, Scotelli gave his partner a quick nod. Rainer took half a step forward to place his gun against Bobby Colville's head and then pulled the trigger. The kid's skull blew apart like a ripe melon and his now flabby body dropped to the ground.

Orville's eyes slammed shut as his knees gave out beneath him. When he landed, most of the air got knocked from his lungs. Even so, he managed somehow to desperately push the words from his mouth. "There . . . was . . . a telegram."

"So?"

"Styles . . . he gave me . . . your money . . . didn't tell me it was short. Please . . . I don't know anything else."

"And what about this telegram?"

"Said the . . . said to call Bobby home after next job. Said you two were through."

Holstering his gun, Scotelli bent down to grab Orville by the collar and lift him roughly to his feet.

"Oh, we ain't done, old man" he said while shoving the old man toward the cabin. "Not by a long shot."

THIRTEEN

Clint took his time looking around the Prairie Dog Saloon before heading toward the dining area. Overall, the place was quite impressive. Besides the drinking and gambling, the stage shows ran steadily after sundown and the smell coming from the kitchen was enough to make his stomach growl in anticipation.

Still, what struck him most was how rarely the customers got out of line. When a fight did break out, which was rare for a place of its size, the scuffle never went past a few clumsily thrown fists or the occasional shove before the fight was taken outside by a set of beefy knee-breakers. Even then, Clint waited for the sounds of gunfire and was surprised when it never came.

As much as he wanted to sit down to a few hands of poker, Clint couldn't help but distrust the dealers. They just had a certain shiftiness about them that set his gambler's senses on alert. Besides, his stomach wouldn't allow him to stay away from the dining area any longer. When he walked into a section of tables set off to the side of the stage where food was being served, he was unable to spot an empty chair.

"Ready to eat?" a voice asked as if coming from nowhere.

Clint turned to spot a young girl in her late teens dressed in the white apron of every other Prairie Dog employee.

"I'm actually waiting for someone," he said while looking around for Maddy.

"I know, and I've already got a table for you and Miss Lowell. Right this way."

The girl took Clint by the elbow and moved her way expertly through the masses of people. She led him to a small round table in a corner near the kitchen and waited for him to sit. "She told me to tell you to wait right here. You want a drink?"

"Just water would be nice," he said, wanting to keep his wits about him when he started in on his questions.

"I'll bring it over. Just wave me down if you need anything." And before Clint could respond, she was gone, swallowed up into the noise and commotion.

Clint waited for a few minutes and was just beginning to wonder whether or not he'd be dining alone when Maddy sidled up to his table with a mug in one hand and a pitcher of water in the other. Her dress looked even more rumpled than when she'd tossed it onto the floor, and her hair showed every bit of the tussling it had gotten in his bed.

"Water?" she asked sarcastically. "I'd have pegged you as a whiskey drinker."

She sat down and poured his drink. Before he could have a sip, Maddy dipped her fingers into his cup and dabbed them onto her tongue. "I also pegged you for a steak man, so I already ordered it. Hope you don't mind."

"Not at all," Clint said. "So how long has this place been running? I passed through this town a few years ago, and it wasn't anything like this."

"Oh, this saloon's been here since the old days, but it wasn't anything like this. Not until the Three Aces opened up across town."

"That's the place on Main Street?"

"Yep." When she nodded, Maddy's eyes caught the light as though she owned it. The silver streak in her hair winked playfully from behind her ear. "Ulrich—that's the owner—opened up Three Aces and nearly put every other saloon out of business. Every other place except for this one, that is. No, the Prairie Dog prospered enough to give that other hole across town a run for its money."

"That hole seemed to be doing pretty well when I passed by."

"Did you go inside?"

"No. Just passed by on my way here."

"Well, I said it before, and I'll say it again. You made the right choice, Clint."

At first, Clint was surprised to hear her call him by name since he'd never actually told it to her. Then he remembered signing the register when they'd first met. "Wasn't there any trouble to begin with from this Ulrich? I mean, when your boss didn't go out of business and became competition for him, did Ulrich take it in stride?"

"It wasn't easy, but competition did me wonders. All the others packed their bags and left just like that," she said while snapping her fingers. From the corner of his eye, Clint could see two servers looking up at the sound she made.

"But not me," she continued. "I love competition just as much as Ulrich."

Suddenly, Clint realized he'd had the wrong impression of Maddy Lowell. "You're not just the hostess are you?" he asked.

"I told you that awhile ago."

"Sure, but you didn't tell me that you owned the place."

She nodded demurely as if trying to look surprised at that statement.

Clint, on the other hand, wouldn't let her get away with it. "Come on, Maddy. You know an awful lot about how this place works to be just someone who works here. And I've never seen dealers and serving girls flinch when one of their own snapped their fingers like that."

"Not only do I own this place, but I made it into something that's giving jobs to half the people in this town."

"While Ulrich takes care of the other half."

Maddy chewed on that for a second while the serving girl brought over a thick steak for Clint and a bowl of soup for her. "So what's with all the questions about my business?" she asked without waiting for the server to clear out of earshot. "I thought you were just here for a good time like everyone else."

Now it was Clint's turn to let the conversation hang for a

little while. Casually he tasted his food and washed it down with a few swallows of coppery well water. Maddy simply watched him as the soup cooled off in front of her. His mind was racing as he thought about what Edgar had said concerning someone trying to take over his saloon and that that someone had been from Mandrake.

His first notion was that a prosperous businessman with thoughts of expanding would have more than enough reason to move in on a small-timer like Edgar. Still, he didn't see why someone would leave a place like Mandrake for a dirt-poor settlement like Wayne, Nebraska. Now that he knew Maddy was one of the prosperous business owners he'd been suspecting, he didn't quite know what to think.

"You thinking of expanding anytime soon?" Clint asked while keeping the suspicion from showing on his face.

Again, Maddy nodded. "Maybe even setting up somewhere else. Some other town, you know? Some place I wouldn't have to worry about the likes of Ulrich or the Three Aces taking away so much of my profits."

And there it was.

With those last words, Maddy had told Clint enough to make him think that she might actually have something to gain from the fire in Wayne after all. If she couldn't get a hold of Edgar's place or the hotel, the next thing to do in order to make sure she'd have no competition would be to get rid of both businesses altogether. Mandrake hadn't been much of a town either until the deluxe saloon started bringing in the customers, so why not try the same thing again with another small town?

As much as he hated to admit it, Clint was starting to see the possibility of something darker lurking behind Maddy's pretty face. But something else told him to hold off before coming to any conclusions. There was still another half of the puzzle he needed to see.

"Is something wrong, Clint? You seem awful quiet."

"Nothing's wrong. Just thinking things over."

"Well, I need to get back to work." Getting up, she walked behind Clint and ran her hands along his shoulders while leaning down to whisper in his ear. "Maybe I'll come tuck you in later."

"Better not, Maddy," he said, putting a regretful tone in his voice, "I've got a long couple of days ahead of me."

FOURTEEN

When Clint walked out of the Prairie Dog, he felt as if he'd been hiding away from the rest of the world. The stars were out, and they stretched overhead, making the sky look like a dark blanket with pinholes in it. Third Street was lit by several lanterns hanging from posts placed every ten feet or so, casting a dull glow on all the cathouses and the occasional opium den.

Crossing over toward the other part of the town, he saw an immediate change in his surroundings as the lamplight gave way to cool darkness. Shops were closed up and lifeless except for the few that doubled as homes for their owners and even those only showed a single flickering light on a few of the upper levels.

For the most part, Mandrake was asleep. If Clint concentrated enough to block out the voices echoing from the saloon district, he could even picture what the town was like before cards and liquor became its primary source of income. All that came to an end once he got closer to Main Street.

Once there, the noises started getting louder and the crowds began sprouting up again. He could see a few differences, though. Where most of the people milling about near the Prairie Dog were wild drunkards howling at the moon, the people Clint was finding in this area seemed slightly more refined. At least they weren't parading with a bottle in one hand and a prostitute in the other.

If Mandrake, Iowa, could have much of an upper social class, the crowd walking down Main Street would be it. Dressed in clothes they'd at least taken the time to clean, the people here were older and on their way out to one of several theaters or social clubs, which all seemed to be radiating out from the hub of a single saloon.

The Three Aces.

It was roughly the same size as the Prairie Dog, but with a more polished appearance. Most of the building was contained in two levels, but a third could be seen sitting on top of it all. From where Clint was, he guessed the third level to be about the size of a small cabin and didn't appear to be occupied at the moment. Black and gold banners had been hung from the edge of the roof and a thick murmur of conversation emanated from inside.

Although the crowd around here had a different feel to it, they were still out to have a night on the town and didn't mind letting everyone else know about it. One of the bigger theaters had just let out and most of the couples who'd attended the performance were making their way straight to the Three Aces. Clint decided to join them.

Just like the Prairie Dog, the Three Aces was in good repair and filled to bursting with customers. The more Clint walked around the saloon, the more he wondered where the hell all these people were coming from. Mandrake had grown since the last time he'd been there, but it still didn't seem big enough to pack not only one, but two giant saloons to capacity.

Essentially, the Three Aces had most everything the Prairie Dog had, only in a slightly better quality. The gambling tables were covered with a felt that wasn't quite as faded. The food smelled of herbs and spices whose names Clint couldn't quite remember. The singers on the stage were crooning in French and Italian. Even the bottles lining the back of the bar seemed to be made of a finer glass, or crystal in some cases.

Clint walked up to the bar and put his foot on the brass rail, which ran along the bottom. The bartender, like all the other employees, was wearing a red shirt and black vest. When he stepped up to Clint, he didn't say hello or even ask for an order. Instead, he just stood there, looking fancy in his spotless uniform.

"Whiskey," Clint said. For some reason, Edgar's moonshine had given him a taste for whiskey, when most of the time he usually drank beer.

The bartender turned and plucked a crystal container from the counter behind him and tipped a portion of liquor into a shot glass. After setting it in front of Clint, he turned and took care of the fellow next down the row.

Sipping the drink, Clint got an even better feel for the difference between both saloons. While the overall quality of the Three Aces was better, it lacked a certain presence that coursed through every plank of the Prairie Dog. The whiskey was smooth and warm, but the place itself seemed a little cold.

Clint took his drink in hand and went on a walking tour of the rest of the place. One thing that was definitely in the Three Aces' favor was the feel of its poker tables. Having handled more than his fair share of cards in his day, Clint had a sixth sense when it came to how a table was being run and how experienced the dealer was at his craft.

He wasn't dumb enough to put his money down on any of the Prairie Dog's tables for fear of getting it swindled out from under him. This was different. As soon as he found an empty chair, Clint sat down in it and bought into a game. At least if any of these people were cheating, they were a whole lot better at it than the ones in Maddy's place. Clint was a firm believer in skill overcoming dishonesty, and two-bit hustlers were more likely to pull a gun than a king from their sleeve. The sharps could be handled without so much dramatics.

He started out small, putting only enough to cover the ante and a few bets in front of him at the table. Throwing away a seven of hearts, Clint sat back and waited for the dealer to give him a spade and fill in his flush. When he got another heart, Clint was glad he hadn't done much by way of raising during the first round of betting.

Apparently, he wasn't the only one starting out small. The other three players and the dealer went around for only two sets of raises, which Clint wanted no part of since he had a whole lot of nothing in his hand. Even the lowest hand on the table, which turned out to be a pair of sevens, would have sent him packing. The game went to a skinny man on his right who wound up with two kings.

Clint used his time during that first hand to get a better feel for the men he was playing with. The dealer was an average-looking man in his forties with a thin mustache and a bald scalp. He wore the black vest of all the other workers there, but with a black armband that was specific to the saloon's dealers.

Normally, Clint didn't like to engage in much conversation when he gambled, but he was here for something more than a game. He struck up some of the small talk that he normally wanted to avoid and found the other players were just as receptive as he would usually be. They answered his questions and were courteous enough, but weren't there to talk.

The man on his right who'd won that last hand was a banker on his way back from California. Sitting directly across from Clint was Bennett, a tall barrel-chested miner on his way to the Black Hills, and next to him was one of the workers for the local telegraph office. Most everyone called that one Reed because he looked like he would snap in half if someone walked past him too quickly. Clint introduced himself as well, but left out his last name to avoid all the questions that would raise. None of the others seemed to miss it.

The next hand was dealt, and Clint got an uneasiness that he couldn't quite explain. It certainly had nothing to do with his hand, which had no possibilities whatsoever beyond a queen high. There was something about the players.

It was something that had drawn him to the table in the first place, and he didn't recognize it even through the first round of betting. When he got his three fill-in cards, Clint wound up with an ace and nothing much else.

The betting this time went hot and heavy, making it certain in Clint's mind that at least one or two of them had actually gotten what they'd needed. When it came down to Bennett and the banker, the bets began to skyrocket until Bennett just called, laying down his kings and nines.

"So what do you have?" Bennett asked.

The banker leaned forward, scraped in his chips, and dropped three eights on the table. "Sorry, friend, but luck was smiling on me."

Just then, Clint noticed something. It was just barely visible when the banker moved his chair and stood up to leave. It was the edge of a playing card. Clint didn't even have to see it to know that it was the card that belonged in the banker's hand instead of one of those eights.

"I don't think I ever caught your name," Clint said as he rose to accompany the man in the well-tailored business suit.

"Sorry," the banker huffed. "It's Kenneth Styles. If you'll excuse me, I really do have an appointment to keep."

I'll bet you do, Clint thought as he watched the other man leave.

FIFTEEN

The cabin along the banks of the Platte River had been gutted until it was an empty shell. Shuffling along pulling a singed wooden cart was a solitary mule with fear in its eyes, but not enough energy to run. Inside the empty cabin, there was a body savaged beyond all recognition; that had been cut to pieces until there was nothing left but mush. A chair that the corpse had been tied to was all that kept it upright.

A few miles up the river, Scotelli and Rainer rode in silence. Neither man had said a word since the fire had started. Rainer knew better than to speak until the other man was ready. Anything sooner would just result in a fight.

Finally, when the smell of bloody flesh was no longer in the air, Rainer couldn't wait any longer. "I suppose the old man talked," he said to break the quiet.

"Yeah, he talked all right."

"You gonna tell me, or do I have to guess?"

Scotelli laughed under his breath, picturing something that Rainer would never want to even think about. "He told me to stop punching him in the face and cutting his skin off."

Rainer had killed plenty of men. He'd even killed a few women in his day, but none of them were fun for him. He'd been working with Pete Scotelli for a long enough time to see the Italian do things that would make even the hardest killer think about finding another line of work. Although they made a good team, Rainer didn't much care for his partner. And he never liked watching him indulge himself on the job.

Trying not to imagine if Scotelli was kidding or not, Rainer held back a shudder. "I trust he told you something that was worth me killing that boy?"

"You never liked that kid."

"True enough."

"The money was short, George. That's more'n enough reason to kill that little shit heel." Looking over to the other man, Scotelli spoke in a conspiratorial whisper. "They was gonna kill us."

"They couldn't have killed us. Not even if they tried."

"Don't be an idiot! You know as well as I do that the people that do more killin' are them that hire the killers. We wouldn't have half the ghosts on our conscience if we weren't paid to do it."

Rainer doubted if the pay was Scotelli's only reason for the murders he'd committed, but he understood the point being made. "So they put a price on our heads?"

"Why else would they call off that little sissy-boy watchdog of theirs unless they was about to cut us loose? That kid's been with us for every job we did for Ulrich, no exceptions. Now, on the day before our biggest job, you hear he's about to get sent home."

"How much was in the bags?" Rainer asked.

Scotelli spit the answer out like it tasted bad. "Not even half. Hell, it was like he wanted us to kill them."

At the same time, both men stopped their horses and turned to face each other. The feeling between them was thick enough to weigh their shoulders down.

Thinking over all that had happened in the last few hours and then over the last few days, Rainer found the truth in everything his partner had just said. They'd been following around in Styles's footsteps for just under a month and across two states. The money from all their jobs had been coming from someone named Ulrich who'd insisted Bobby Colville come along to make sure the hired guns didn't get out of line.

The cash had always been on time and perfectly counted and the jobs had been flowing one after another. Until now. Neither of the men had had much in the way of schooling, but they knew well enough how a con job worked.

"I'll bet you're thinkin' the same thing I am," Scotelli said.

"Only if you think we need to find Styles before he skips town with our money."

Scotelli nodded while his face twisted into a hateful mask. "That son of a bitch had to know we'd kill whoever tried to short us! That's why he picked this time to send someone else with the money instead of bringin' it, himself."

"But why now?" Rainer asked.

"Couldn't tell you. But I can think of one skinny little weasel in a suit who can."

Without needing to say another word, both men put the spurs to their horses and headed north.

When they arrived in Omaha, they made straight for the hotel that Kenneth Styles called home. Scotelli jumped off his horse the instant he was in sight of the place and stormed inside. As he did when on any other job, Rainer waited outside, ready to deal with any trouble moving in behind Scotelli or any coming out when he left.

The hotel used to belong to a family that had lived in Omaha since the town was nothing but a wide spot in the road. One of Styles's first jobs was to convince the owner to sell, which they did since they were ready to leave for Wyoming anyway. If they hadn't, Styles was set to burn it down.

Even now, walking into the lobby, Scotelli could still remember where they'd planned to pour the kerosene. "Where's Styles?" he roared to the surprised young man behind the front desk.

"Mister Styles left."

"When?"

"Yesterday. Please, Mister Scotelli, you're upsetting the customers."

Scotelli pulled his gun and jammed it beneath the desk clerk's chin. "Tell me where he went, or I'll upset the brains in your fool head!"

"I'm really not supposed to—"

Scotelli clicked back the hammer of his forty-five. The clerk's eyes crossed, looking straight to the gun. The sight would have made Scotelli laugh if not for his foul mood.

"Mandrake," the younger man spat out. "Mandrake, Iowa. He took the first stage out of town and should be there by now."

"He leave any messages?"

"No. He didn't leave anything at all."

Wheeling around toward the door, Scotelli came face to face with a pair of extremely nervous customers. He holstered his gun and took off out the door. "Hope you're ready for a ride," he said once he saddled up. "Because we're heading out."

As usual, Rainer slowed his pace to make sure they wouldn't be followed before turning his back on the hotel and catching up with his partner. He'd seen the look in Scotelli's eyes and knew there would be no talking to him for a while longer.

That suited him just fine since they both wanted the same thing: to get their hands on the rest of their money as well as the double-crosser who'd tried to cheat them out of it.

SIXTEEN

Clint was given a complete tour of the Three Aces Saloon simply by keeping a few steps behind Kenneth Styles as the banker made his rounds from the poker tables to the bar and to a table near the stage. With a crowd that seemed big enough to account for half the town, Clint had no trouble at all going unnoticed.

Now, he was waiting to see if the banker would be able to show him anything else before Clint confronted him directly. Namely, Clint was waiting to see if Styles would be able to introduce him to this Ulrich he'd been hearing about recently. More than likely, that was the man who'd backed Styles and his firebugs.

Which meant that Ulrich was the main man Clint was after.

"Can I help you?" came a smooth, silken voice from the crowd.

Clint turned quickly to see who'd spoken while trying to keep Styles in the corner of his eye. What he found was a tall blond in a formfitting dress made of a black, lacy material that accentuated a trim yet well-sculpted figure. Her skin had been darkly bronzed by the sun, which made her hair appear to gleam in the dim lighting of the saloon. She looked at Clint with gentle blue eyes while holding out a hand to make sure he didn't bump into one of the other guests.

"You seem like you're looking for someone," she said with full, luscious lips. "Maybe I can help you."

Clint turned quickly to find Styles had seated himself at a table near the stage and appeared to be settling in for a French cancan number. "Actually, I was looking for somewhere to sit."

"Tonight's one of our busiest nights, but I'll see what I can do." With a swift waving motion, she called over one of the numerous workers in black vests, who pointed toward the back of the room.

"Looks like the only thing left is in the back," she said. "I'll show you."

Clint's first reaction was to refuse the offer and stay close to Styles, but when the blond took his hand in hers, he couldn't bring himself to pull away. Her touch was firm, yet warm, her hands wrapped in soft black lace. What clinched the deal was when she stepped in front of him to move toward the table. She wore her hair mostly up, but with a few thick strands dangling to the open neckline of her dress, revealing the upper slope of breasts that looked just as soft as the rest of her.

"I don't know if I have the time to—" Then he caught the faint scent of roses coming from her hair. The next thing he knew, Clint was sitting at a small table in the back of the room.

It wasn't the best view in the place, but Clint could still occasionally make out Styles's back when enough people moved out of the way. Over in that section of the large room, the lights dimmed and the curtain went up. A line of chorus girls danced onto the stage and began kicking in time to the music.

"Did you want something to eat or are you just here for the show?" the gorgeous blond asked.

Satisfied that Styles wasn't going anywhere, Clint allowed himself to give his full attention over to the stunning hostess. "I haven't been in this town for a full day yet, and I've had more people trying to take care of me than I know what to do with."

"This town is built around its entertainment. Most of the people in it are only here for a few days or a week at the most. Those people are our bread and butter. We take care of those people. It's their money that puts food on the tables of those of us who have grown up in Mandrake."

Just listening to her talk was enough to make Clint forget about nearly everything else around him. The way her head moved just enough to make the wisps of hair dance around her face. The motion of her soft, moist lips as they formed the words.

"Please," he said, "have a seat. You must be tired from looking after those people all day long."

A bright smile shone on her face, followed by a melodious laugh. "Actually, I don't mind if I do."

When she got off her feet, she stretched her arms out to the sides luxuriously as if she couldn't remember a time when she wasn't standing. Her hands came down to smooth out her dress, making sure most of it was out of the way and would not get too trampled.

"Been a long day?" he asked.

"It does feel good to sit still for a minute." She closed her eyes and leaned her head back, rolling some of the kinks out of her neck. When she opened them again, she waved to a bartender and asked for some water for them both.

"I won't stay long," she said apologetically. "I'm sure you're probably meeting someone or have something planned for your evening."

"Actually, I'd like it if you stayed. My name's Clint." He reached across the table, hoping to feel her smooth hand take hold of his.

She clasped his hand immediately. "I'm Greta."

"So what do you do here?"

"Pretty much what I did for you. Move around, make sure everyone's doing alright."

"I've been to more saloons than I can count, and I've never been taken care of like I am at the ones in this town."

Greta's smile turned down a little at the edges. "So you've already been to another part of town?"

"Yes. The Prairie Dog. It's not quite as nice as this place but"—he thought back to his steamy encounter with Maddy and couldn't help but feel a flush of excitement—"it did have its own unique charm."

"Well, if you'd stayed there too long, that charm would have worn off. I can tell just by looking at you that you've got too much taste to want to spend your time in a bawdy house like that."

"Funny, but I see a lot of the same things here as I did there. In fact, apart from some of the fancy decorations, this place is almost identical."

"Well, the Prairie Dog is nothing but a copy of this establishment." Greta felt a tap on her shoulder. When she turned around, the bartender was there with a pitcher of water and two glasses. She leaned back and let him do the pouring. He was done quickly and went back to his bar.

Clint couldn't help but admire the way Greta's body curved when she moved.

"I'm sure you're not here to talk about the saloon business," she said after taking a long sip.

"I'd love to talk about other things, Greta, if you'd like to meet me after you're done working."

Her body language and expression showed a reflexive response to all the countless offers she would have to endure in her line of work. But then she softened again and nodded curtly. "I believe I would like that. Are you staying here?"

"I . . . don't have a room yet."

"Well, sign in at the far end of the bar, and I'll find you in a few hours."

"I'm looking forward to it."

Now it was her who reached across the table for his hand. The movement brought Clint closer to her rose-scented hair and that rich, darkened skin. "Likewise," she said.

SEVENTEEN

Having been drinking for the better part of two days, Red was more than earning his name. His skin was flushed, and his eyes looked more sunken than usual with bright bloody streaks crisscrossing the whites. After one of his best gun hands had been killed in Wayne, Red had learned the value of being a bit more careful in his rages.

But careful or not, his rage was unmistakable. Any man could see it brewing behind those tired eyes just as they could see it in the way he carried himself as if looking for any excuse at all to draw his pistol.

Sitting in the back of the Prairie Dog Saloon, he nursed another bottle of warm beer while considering his options. He could go out and try and find the stranger who'd killed his man. Although he didn't expect to run into him here in Mandrake, Red was more than willing to accept his luck for what it was and take his revenge when he could.

Or, he could wait and meet with the person who'd sent him to Wayne in the first place. That was the main reason why he'd come back to Iowa at all. Since he wasn't able to do what needed to be done in Wayne before the whole place was burned down around him.

Once again, everything came back to that stranger who'd shot down one of the men he'd been riding with for the last two years.

Red stood up from his table and shoved his way through the late-night crowd. The constant music and loud voices were getting on his nerves, making him itch for the feel of a gun in his hand just so he could make at least one of those voices stop. He made his way past the gambling tables and roulette wheels, past the kitchen, and to the desk where the keys were handed out for the rooms upstairs.

Maddy wasn't there. In her place was one of the bartenders who looked relieved to get one of the more relaxing jobs in the place for a while. Paying no mind to the man behind the desk, Red grabbed the register and spun it around. "Who's the asshole that checked in earlier tonight?" he asked.

The man in the white apron was used to dealing with the rude ones and simply shrugged his shoulders. "Don't know who you're talking about, mister. You need a room?"

There it was, what Red had been waiting for all along. The gun was out and in the bartender's face before the other man could drop his shoulders.

"Think real hard," Red hissed. "Maddy took him upstairs herself. The whole damn place heard her screamin', so you know damn well who I'm talkin' about."

The bartender was used to the sight of guns as well, but most people could never get used to having one pointed at them. "Oh . . . I think I remember now. He's in room number eight."

Red scanned the register until he came to room eight and read the name that had been signed. He recognized it immediately.

"Clint Adams," he said to himself. "Ain't that just perfect?"

The bartender behind the counter was starting to say something, but Red didn't bother listening. Instead, he flipped the register closed and walked toward the stairs. He knew the Prairie Dog like the back of his hand and didn't even have to look at the numbers on the doors to know when he was approaching The Gunsmith's room.

Thoughts of the fame waiting for him on the other side of that door were all that were going through his mind as he readied his gun and sent a boot crashing into the wood next to the handle. It gave way easily and the door flew inward to slam noisily against the wall.

Red already had the trigger halfway pulled when he noticed the room was empty. He knew better than to look for Adams in any hiding place. After all, The Gunsmith was not one for crawling under beds or running from a fight. At least, not The Gunsmith he'd heard tales of. But just to be sure, Red gave the room a quick once-over before stepping back into the hall.

It didn't matter to him that he'd missed Adams this time since there would be plenty of other times to plan for. His head was still swimming when he walked down the stairs, much to the displeasure of the bartender who'd been more than happy to see him leave.

"If you need something, perhaps I can help you rather than you kicking down our doors," the worker said in exasperation.

"I need a room, after all. Number nine."

The bartender looked for the key and was relieved to find it on the pegboard. He all but threw it at the other man. "There. Now go and cool your heels before you hurt someone."

Red's mood had improved greatly in the last few minutes. Otherwise, he would have smacked the bartender in the mouth for talking to him like he was just another one of the rowdies that lived on his feet at the Prairie Dog's bar.

Before heading back upstairs, Red turned and walked behind the counter until he was toe to toe with the worker there. "One more thing," Red snarled. "You don't say a word about me or anything I done to the man in room number eight. You got that?"

The bartender found himself on familiar territory and held his hand palm up in front of him. "You can get anything you need at the Prairie Dog, but nothing's for free."

"Yeah . . . nothin' but your whore of an owner. How 'bout this . . . I figure one bullet costs me three or four cents, and that's what I'll pay you if you do say anything. And pull that bony little hand back, 'cause when I pay you, I'll put those few cents through your damn head and out the other side."

Slowly, almost timidly, the bartender eased his hand closed and hid it under the counter. "Understood. Have a pleasant stay."

Red next went up the stairs to sit in his room and listen for footsteps in the hallway. When he heard the ones that stopped at room number eight, he would no longer have to take the piss-poor jobs with the piss-poor wages. He could start demanding real money when people wanted to hire his gun, and he could get the respect he'd never had previously.

Famous killers could do that sort of thing.

Especially the one that killed The Gunsmith.

EIGHTEEN

The trail between Omaha and Mandrake was not a long one. It would normally take the better part of a day for a stage to cover the distance, but for a horse riding at full speed with a man who didn't care about its welfare at the reins, the trip was half that.

Scotelli whipped his mare like it had committed a crime, and even when the animal's breaths started coming in ragged, foaming heaves, he barely noticed. Rainer was a bit more fond of his spotted gelding, so he let his partner pull ahead. Besides, he knew that with Scotelli in the mood he was in, finding him would be no problem once they got to town.

It was getting on to midnight when Scotelli rode into Mandrake. He instinctively went to the livery, but even he could tell he should have stopped directly at a vet's office.

"That horse needs a doctor, mister," Arlen said while rubbing his eyes. He normally didn't stay at the stables this late, but he was sleeping off an overdose of whiskey and decided he'd save his wife the trouble of kicking him out.

The olive-skinned rider let his mount drop to the ground after taking what he needed from its saddlebags. "Keep it," Scotelli said.

Arlen shook his head and watched as the man walked off toward the commotion of Main Street. Looking at the poor horse that had already closed its eyes and drifted to sleep, Arlen longed for the days when Mandrake had been smaller. It had also been much poorer, but at least it didn't attract a crowd that lived for nothing but the night life.

"Damn shame," he said while kneeling down to clean the horse's muzzle. "At least you're still breathin'. Let's get you inside."

It took Arlen the better part of an hour before he could convince the exhausted animal into one of the stalls. And just as he'd gotten himself squared away and back to sleep, there was another set of hooves pounding toward him.

Clint and Greta talked on and off for most of the night. His eyes grew tired right along with the rest of his body, but she seemed somehow to maintain her soft-spoken brightness that radiated through every graceful move as she walked around the enormous saloon to tend to her duties, only to come back and talk with him some more.

"It's getting late," she said after two in the morning.

Clint stretched his back and drained the last of several cups of coffee. "I was beginning to think you never got tired."

"It will hit me as soon as I get out of this dress and climb into bed." As if realizing what she'd said, Greta blushed and laughed nervously. "Sorry. I'm talking to you like you work here."

"That's fine by me. I was just thinking about that very thing."

Greta tried to look offended by his forwardness, but couldn't quite pull it off. "I'd better let you find your own way upstairs," she said, "because something tells me you need your rest."

Clint stood up and tried to remember where he was supposed to sleep. After a while, he couldn't tell where he was or how late it had become. Judging by the crowd, it could have been any time of day, and he wasn't close enough to the door to tell if the sun had come out yet.

"A good night's sleep does sound like what I need," he said while following Greta through the crowd and toward the stairs. She looked like she was about to say something in reply, but was cut short by something going on at the bar.

Clint shoved through the milling groups of drinkers until he was closer to the front door. The sky was still black, which gave him some perspective of the hour.

"Where's Ulrich?" a voice boomed from the head of the bar.

Some of the bartenders were trying to calm the man down, but weren't having much success.

"Maybe I should see what he wants," Greta said as she straightened up and put on her best accommodating smile.

Clint grabbed her by the elbow with just enough strength to hold her back. "I don't know about that. Maybe you should just let someone toss him out."

But it was too late. The crowd had moved away from the ranting man just enough for him to see Greta walking up.

This time, when he spoke, it was directly to her. "You in charge here?"

"I can help you if that's what you need," she said in her best hostess voice.

"What I need is a meet with Ulrich. I heard he owns this shit hole."

"If you'd just calm down, I can—"

Clint recognized the violent glint in the man's eyes and stopped Greta from saying another word. Although his interruption seemed to annoy her, he was paying too much attention to the olive-skinned man to notice her reaction. There were several large men wearing black vests walking toward the bar, but Clint had learned a long time ago not to put his life in anyone's hands but his own.

"Maybe you should just leave," he said to the wild-eyed Italian.

Scotelli glared around the place, feeling his rage surge through him like a thunderstorm. Some of the saloon's bouncers were working their way toward him, but he didn't fret them too much. It was the man standing next to the blond that concerned him more. The way that one's hand hung steady over his gun told Scotelli he knew how to use it. Call it instinct. One killer to another.

"This ain't your business," Scotelli warned, "unless your name's Ulrich."

"I've got business with Ulrich, too," Clint said as Greta

turned and looked at him with surprise written across her face. "So let's find him together before we both get thrown out of here."

Although the saloon was far from quiet, the activity in the immediate vicinity had come to a standstill. Scotelli considered his position for a few seconds before shifting on his feet. The movement was slight, but enough to show his shoulders and arms had lost some of the tension from before. His face brightened somewhat as his hands dropped to his sides.

"Does he owe you money, too?" Scotelli asked.

Clint relaxed his guard somewhat, but not enough to give the other man any notions of safety. "No, but he does owe me an explanation."

"First of all," Greta said as she stepped up to stand between them. "I am not a *he*. And second, I doubt if I owe either one of you much of anything."

NINETEEN

Between both men, Clint was the most surprised. He kept quiet, however, until Greta led them both to an office in the back of the hotel desk. The room seemed especially big since the door leading to it was narrower than a closet's. Inside, there was a single lamp with a dark green shade and a large oak desk that was covered with papers, pens, and even a telegraph. When she closed the door, all the noise from the outside seemed to be shut away.

"You're Ulrich?" Clint asked after she'd moved around to sit behind the large desk.

"That's right. Greta Ulrich. Why are you so amazed?"

"Because I've been talking to you all night, and you never mentioned it."

"You never told me your last name," she stated simply. "And you never asked me mine."

"Maybe not, but I know I mentioned that I wanted to talk to Ulrich while I was here, and you still didn't say anything."

"A woman in my position quickly learns to get as much information as she can when dealing in a man's world. I was going to tell you . . . but I figured I'd wait until I knew everything you wanted."

Scotelli stood in front of the door with his arms folded imperiously over his chest. "So you're the only Ulrich in town?" he asked without trying to hide the contempt in his voice.

Looking at him and then back at Clint, Greta held out her hands and shook her head. "See what I mean?"

Scotelli bolted forward and slammed both fists on her desk. "I was the one talkin' to you! Now answer my damn question."

"Yes, I'm the only Ulrich in town. How many more were you expecting?"

"I just needed to know who was responsible for cheatin' me and my partner out of the money you owe us for a job that's already done."

Just then a look of recognition lit up her face. "Ahh, so that must make you Pete Scotelli."

"That's right."

"Mister Styles has returned already, and he told me he sent you your money."

"Yeah . . . half of it. And that's just enough to get someone hurt . . . mainly the one that's got the other half."

Clint was watching the two talk, ready for action if things got too heated. At the moment, however, he wasn't sure which person he should help.

"Mister Scotelli," Greta said in a calm, level voice, "the report I heard from Bobby told me that the job was a lot messier than what I had wanted. You were sent with specific instructions, and you went way over the limits we discussed."

"We ain't never discussed a thing!"

"That was Bobby's job, and he speaks for me, that's why he was—"

"That sissy kid's dead." The words slipped out of Scotelli like cold poison. He spoke them just loud enough to be heard and just soft enough to stop Greta in midsentence.

Clint had heard more than enough. "Alright, now you need to start explaining this to me."

Greta kept her eyes trained on Scotelli. Her face had gone pale, and her lips drew into tight lines. "Bobby Colville represented me on certain assignments."

"He was a pain in me and my partner's ass," Scotelli said. "He got your telegram by the way." Pointing to the little machine sitting on a small round table by the wall, he walked past Clint. "Is that when you told him to short our pay, or did he know about that all along?"

Looking down to her folded hands, Greta seemed either unwilling or unable to continue the conversation.

Clint was more than happy to pick up the slack. "How about you answer me one question," he said to Scotelli. "Was this job anywhere near Wayne, Nebraska?"

Greta moved her head slowly up until she was staring once again at Scotelli. They both held each other's gaze for a few seconds until the Italian wheeled around to stick a finger in Clint's face.

"You need to know when to shut yer mouth!" Scotelli growled. "This ain't none of yer—"

"Yes, Clint," Greta interrupted. "The job was in Wayne, and it went terribly wrong."

Now Clint swung around to stare angrily at the woman sitting behind the desk. "I suppose you know that the job you hired them to do cost a lot of people their homes and businesses and one man his life. I was there, and I'm real surprised that more people didn't die when their town went up in flames."

Her eyes closed, and it was obviously an effort for her to keep the tears from flowing down her cheeks. "How do you know about all this?" she asked.

"I told you. I was there. I was in the hotel when the fire started and wound up spending the night tearing down an entire camp before everything in it was lost. I suppose you know who Kenneth Styles is."

Scotelli reared back as if something had bit him on the nose. "Is that bastard here, too?" He slapped his hands together and rubbed them in anticipation. "Because that would save me another trip."

Clint and Greta ignored the other man. They were too busy trying to get a better handle on the confusion that had been thrust upon them the instant that office door had closed. Although Clint had thought long and hard about what he would do when he found whoever was responsible for the fire in Wayne, he never even dreamed he'd be considering giving them a second chance.

Something seemed wrong with the way Greta was reacting. Clint had a whole new set of questions for her, but he didn't want Scotelli to be around when he asked them.

"You know what?" Scotelli asked as his hand moved for his gun. "Why don't you just give me the money you owe, plus a little interest besides, and I'll take care of Styles when I catch up to him."

With his nerves already on edge, Clint only needed to catch the hint of the other man moving toward his gun to set his reflexes into action.

By the time Scotelli had his hand around the pistol grip and had thumbed back the hammer, Clint had already cleared leather and was positioning himself in front of Greta. All he needed was one clean shot to be able to end the fight before it even started. But Scotelli had purposely slowed his own movements to hide his real speed until the last second before they were needed. It was an old gunfighter's trick, but very effective if pulled off just right.

Scotelli's arm moved at half speed until he'd cocked the pistol. Then, he dove to the side, drawing and firing in one swift motion.

The shot went wild, taking a chunk from the corner of Greta's desk. Clint ducked and fired at the spot where Scotelli had been standing, his bullet missing the other man by less than an inch. Then the door to the office flew open and all hell broke loose.

TWENTY

When the door busted open, it was immediately filled with the hulking figure of one of the Three Aces' bouncers. The man wore a black and white suit, its jacket open to reveal a shoulder rig over a black vest. He had to duck to get in, which lowered the Colt he was holding as he looked over at Greta.

"Are you all right, Miss Ulrich?" the bouncer asked.

Even as Clint was throwing himself at him, Scotelli managed to get a shot off that went over Clint's shoulder and into the bouncer's side. The huge man gripped his ribs and dropped to one knee, squeezing off a shot that whipped over Clint's head and into the wall.

When Clint landed, he swung his pistol up and fired. This time his bullet managed to graze Scotelli as he pressed himself to the floor and started rolling toward the desk.

With the door open, the sound of general panic could be heard coming from the saloon's main room. There were more armed men in black vests struggling to step over the first bouncer, who was doing his best to shuffle to the side and let them pass. The next one entered the office with his head low, which kept it from getting blown off by Scotelli's next shot.

Rather than waste another round, Clint threw himself forward to land on top of Scotelli. His fist made contact before any other part of him hit, catching the Italian square on the jaw. With that one punch, the world seemed to switch into slow motion. Clint could see the other man's gun coming around to point at him, just as he could see the bouncers approaching from the side. The only thing he couldn't see was Greta, which made him want to deal with Scotelli as quickly as possible.

Scotelli's pistol was getting closer, but rather than trying to fire another round, he was swinging high to bash Clint across his left temple. Although shooting him would do more damage, Scotelli had decided to keep surprise on his side and hurt Clint enough by using the gun as a club.

The room was filled with so much noise it made it difficult to concentrate on any single voice. There were bouncers yelling for everyone to get out, there was the roar of the outside crowd, and on top of it all, Clint's ears were still ringing from the gunshots that had exploded within the enclosed space.

Clint reached out to grab for Scotelli's hand before his face was in his line of fire, but the other man seemed to slip from his grasp. The next thing Clint felt was the blinding pain of something hard crashing into his skull, and the lights around him seemed to dim.

Time sped up to normal once again as Clint's back hit the floor. When he shook the cobwebs from his head, he could feel the pounding of Scotelli's body on the floor as the man struggled to his feet, and then dashed for the door. If not for the bouncers clogging the entrance, the Italian would have made it through. However, while the men in black vests were armed, none of them seemed ready to fire.

That didn't hold true for Clint.

His hand moved practically on its own. Clint brought his gun up and around, but didn't have time to line up a shot. Instead, he followed through as if he were simply pointing at Scotelli with his finger and pulled the trigger. Most men wouldn't have been able to hit much else besides the door frame or one of the massive bouncers, but Clint managed to sink a piece of lead into Scotelli's shoulder, which sent him face-first onto the floorboards behind the hotel desk.

Although he was a bit shaky on his feet, Clint stood up and ran for the door. As soon as he had pushed one of the smaller bouncers aside, he heard the crack of a rifle a split second before he felt the hot pain tear through his neck.

In a flash, all of the bouncers had hit the floor and Clint had pulled himself back into the office with his back pressed against the wall next to the door. He quickly reached up to feel the fresh bullet wound, and his fingers came away covered in blood. He'd gotten in the way of enough bullets to know that this one hadn't done any real damage. Luckily, the wound was more of a wide, jagged cut where the bullet had grazed the side of his neck.

"Come on, Pete!" yelled a voice from somewhere near the bar.

Scotelli grinned widely as he scrambled to his feet and headed to where Rainer waited with smoking rifle in hand. They'd worked so long together, Scotelli had known his partner would be ready to cover his back. And once again, Rainer hadn't disappointed him.

All it took was a few shots toward the ceiling to send everyone in the place to the ground. With his hand clamped against the bloody hole that had been torn through his shoulder, Scotelli took off through the front door, holstering his gun when he'd made it outside. Rainer backed down the bar, staring down the barrel of his rifle while levering in a fresh cartridge. Nobody was close enough to make a difference, so once he was outside, Rainer followed in his partner's wake.

"You never want to do anything the easy way," Rainer said once he'd caught up to Scotelli.

Outside the saloon, the rest of the town was fast asleep. There were a few stragglers making their way to or from their next drink, but the law still hadn't quite arrived yet.

"Easy way's too slow. I figure this'll make it worth their while to pay us off and get us out of here."

"You find Ulrich?"

"Yeah. We can take care of her and Styles all at the same time."

"Wait a minute. Ulrich is a her?"

"Let's just get off the street. I'll explain later."

Kenneth Styles sat at his secluded table near the corner of the stage and watched with great amusement as Pete Scotelli and his partner rampaged through the saloon like wild boars. One of the first things he'd learned when he started in his chosen business was to be surprised by nothing.

Surprise wasn't good for anything besides handing over your advantage to someone else and that was always a bad business move. He wasn't even surprised to see one of his former poker partners come charging from Greta's office after Rainer had left.

Everyone around them had stopped their talking and put their drinks down for the first time all night when they'd heard the gunshots. That alone had been a sight to see. Styles had just sipped his brandy and watched the show that had replaced the one on the stage.

Inside, he was refiguring all the angles. He knew Orville was dead, but that was a necessary precaution. Colville was more than likely a casualty as well. Now, with Scotelli spouting off to anyone who would listen, Ulrich would be suspicious and looking for answers. That is, unless she'd been shot in her office.

All in all, this little escapade simply meant he needed to step up his timetable. Greta was supposed to die eventually. Sooner or later, it didn't really matter. As for this new player, Styles recalled he'd said his name was Clint. He really didn't know much more than that.

Styles didn't like not knowing. It would be so much easier just to be rid of him.

Yes, he decided after taking another sip of brandy. Better to be safe and have him killed along with Ulrich when the real professionals came.

TWENTY-ONE

Clint had tried going after Scotelli, only to find the rifleman covering his back. After the other man had left, Clint knew that both of them would have had plenty of time to turn into any one of the alleys or duck into any number of doorways. They were gone. He wasn't going to catch them. Not right now, anyway.

Which left him with some time to deal with Greta Ulrich.

Grabbing a rag from one of the bartenders, Clint pressed it to the wound on his neck and tossed back a shot to dull the pain. He would be needing stitches. The good news was that the town doctor was already in the Three Aces. The bad news was that he'd been there for the better part of the evening. Surprisingly enough, even through the stench of alcohol on the doctor's breath, his hands were quick and steady with the needle and thread.

After his stitches were in, Clint walked back to Greta's office to make sure she was all right. He found her sitting behind her desk, assuring her bouncers and several others of that very thing.

"I told you I'm fine," she said insistently to an older man with a ring of graying hair and a generous paunch. "I'm a little shaken up, but other than that, I'm just fine."

Standing in the door frame, Clint knocked on the wood three

times with his knuckle. Greta seemed happy for someone else to talk to.

"Look, I've still got a business to run," she told her workers. "So start cleaning up and make sure we didn't lose too many guests. And somebody please tell me they got the sheriff."

There were assurances all around. The sheriff was on his way.

After everyone else had filed out, Clint stepped back into the office and shut the door behind him. The wound was really starting to hurt now that the excitement of the gunfight had passed. That, combined with the fatigue from nearly an entire day without sleep made it harder for Clint to stay upright. When he slumped into a small chair facing Greta's desk, Clint knew it was going to be a chore to get back up again.

"I suppose you're going to want some kind of explanation for all of this," Greta said, looking every bit as tired as Clint felt. "Judging by the questions you were asking, it seems like you know a lot of it anyhow."

"I know what happened in Wayne. Why don't you tell me your part in it?"

Greta sighed heavily and rested her forehead on her hands. "You've been to the Prairie Dog, haven't you?"

"Yes."

"Between the owner of that place and myself, we've breathed new life into this town and have become quite well-off in the process. After all the work I've put into my saloon, I can rightly say that I've earned every penny I've got. Still, like any other successful business owner worth their salt, my next step was to expand."

"Expand?" Clint said with a laugh. "What more do you want besides one of the biggest and most profitable saloons I've ever seen. And keep in mind, I've seen an awful lot of them."

"Nobody expected me to do much with my money. Most people thought I'd buy some land and maybe travel for a while. Instead, I built a saloon and dedicated years of my life to making it something to be proud of."

"And where did you get your money?"

"I named this place after the hand I was dealt."

"You won enough to start a business with three aces?"

"It wasn't as impressive as a full house, but it was enough to win a thirty-thousand-dollar pot."

"Fair enough."

Leaning back, Greta seemed to be regaining some of the poise that Clint had admired throughout much of the evening. "Anyway, I took a run-down spider nest of a building and built it up into what you see. It took a lot of years, and in that time, I had to put my business in front of everything else.

"Once I got the know-how, the whole thing seemed so easy. Most people in this town or many of the others around it hadn't seen a saloon done up as much as mine. I put an entire town's worth of entertainment into one building. Then came poker tournaments and all the other games you can imagine. Hostesses, food, drink . . . pretty soon we had people coming in from all the neighboring towns just to stay at my saloon. That allowed me to improve more and so on. I did a lot of good for Mandrake."

"And the Prairie Dog?" he asked.

Suddenly a stern look came across her face, as if it was triggered by the mere mention of the other saloon in town. "Miss Lowell just wants to copy my formula to make herself rich."

"Last I heard, that was a term called *competition* we use in this country," Clint said sarcastically. "And as far as I know, it's perfectly legal."

"Sure," she scoffed, "legal right up to the point when she starts bringing in hired guns to make sure nobody else gets to compete."

Clint's ears perked up at those words. "What hired guns?"

"About a year or so ago, Madeline Lowell started making offers to buy out my saloon. I wasn't interested in selling, and she didn't like that one bit. After a few more offers, she started sending men in to try and persuade me by shooting the place up and breaking windows. You know . . . real *competition.* If I hadn't had enough money to buy my own protection, I would have been out of business—probably out of town—within a week.

"I learned one thing from that woman and that was the notion of going out there and chasing down opportunities for my business."

"I suppose this is the part where you hired your own guns?" Clint asked.

"No. The man I hired was a businessman from New York named Kenneth Styles. He came recommended to me by some friends of mine back East who told me this man was the best at scouting out new territory and that he had an office in Sioux City. I'll tell you something, Clint. If Mister Styles had the skills with a gun he does with fast-talking, he would have been able to give William Bonney a run for his money."

Settling back into her chair, Greta took a deep breath to prepare herself for the next part of her tale. "In short, Mister Styles took my ideas and ran with them. I wanted to open saloons like this one in other towns that would profit from them as much as this one had. He would go to those towns and scout them out, buy land, or make offers to buy existing saloons so we could build them up. Together, we'd set up interests in eight saloons across Iowa, Kansas, and South Dakota. The move into Nebraska was next since a lot of folks still travel through there on their way out to California or Colorado.

"A month ago, I started hearing about businesses being burnt down that I later found out had been ones that Styles was going to approach with an offer. I didn't think much of it until he started buying saloons damaged by fire at a reduced price."

"And you didn't find any of that suspicious?" Clint asked.

She fixed him with a cool, yet troubled stare. It was the face of someone used to being strong. It was also the face of someone trying hard not to break. "All I saw were reports by telegraph about him buying up land and buildings at lower and lower prices. That's why I started sending someone I could trust along with him to keep an eye on what exactly he was doing out there."

"A spy?"

"No. Styles knew I sent Colville along to report back to me. I probably shouldn't have told him so much," she said as her voice dropped, and her eyes began to tear up. "I realized that when Colville was killed by some men Styles had hired as assistants."

Clint didn't like the sound of that. "And these assistants, I suppose they carried guns?"

Greta nodded silently. "Styles said he needed protection. Bobby would send me cables about these men and how they would send him away. Except, on the most recent trip, he'd managed to stay with them and had watched as Styles had made his offer to a local saloon and was turned down. Normally, I would want him to move on and scout out somewhere else we could build. Instead, he threatened this man and finally . . ." Her voice trailed off, and she buried her face in her hands.

Clint stood up and handed over a handkerchief, watching her for any sign that she was playing up her grief just to look innocent in his eyes. "That was in Wayne, wasn't it?"

After dabbing at her eyes, she nodded again. "Yes. I got word from Bobby and told him to come back before he got hurt. I also sent word to Styles that our business was through and that I wouldn't have a part in something so horrible as burning people out of their homes and businesses."

While she seemed genuinely troubled, Clint knew better than to make any snap judgments until he'd heard from every side. "Did you tell the law about him?"

She paused to gather herself. Folding her hands over the kerchief, she looked Clint straight in the eyes and said, "Styles sent his own telegram. He said if I bring in the law, his men would come after me. Now," she said while motioning toward the shot-up door frame, "it looks like he wants me dead anyway."

Clint opened the door. He didn't have enough information to deny what she'd told him, and he couldn't dispute the fact that someone wanted her dead. "That man who shot at us said he wanted the rest of his money," Clint pointed out. "What was he talking about?"

"I honestly don't know. All I do know is that I'm scared of Styles and what he'll do to me."

"Then you should probably know that he was in your saloon today."

"Oh, God. I've got to get him out of here!"

"Before you do that, I'd like to talk to him."

"Please don't. He scares me."

"I honestly don't think he's going to try anything else tonight after his men were driven out of here, and I'll make sure we have our talk somewhere else if it would make you feel better."

"It would, Clint. Thank you." Suddenly, Greta seemed to brighten as she stood and walked over to where he was standing. She wrapped her arms around him and squeezed tightly, almost desperately. "I'm still scared, but I feel so safe after seeing what you did to protect me. You could have been killed."

"A lot better men than that one has tried."

"Still, I wish I could thank you properly for saving my life." When she said those words, her voice lost all its uncertainty and fear. Instead, she was excited by him. Her arousal warmed her hands upon him and had their own effect on Clint's body as well.

"I'll try to help you," he said while trying not to let on how much he wanted her. "Just don't make the mistake in thinking I work for you."

Before she could respond, he pulled away from her and left the office.

TWENTY-TWO

Virtually every other hotel or saloon in Mandrake had either collapsed due to lack of customers or had simply given up trying to compete with the Three Aces and the Prairie Dog. All that was left were a few boardinghouses and small family-run bars that were kept alive by old timers who couldn't take the noise inside the walls of the town's two major drinking halls.

One of these boardinghouses was on the outskirts of town, relatively far enough away from both of the big saloons to be quiet most evenings. In the years since the opening of the Prairie Dog, this particular boardinghouse hadn't seen more than three paying customers. Tonight, their business picked up as two rough-looking men checked in and paid for two nights in advance.

The owner, a gray-haired old woman whose children had long ago picked up and moved south, was so happy, she got right to work baking pies for dessert the following night.

Pete Scotelli stretched out on the soft bed, which came complete with down comforter. Normally, he was used to sleeping on the ground or in whorehouses, neither of which had much by way of comfort. He felt like he was on vacation, even though he was shot.

Gritting his teeth, Scotelli adjusted his position so he wasn't leaning on his wound. It had held together long enough for him to get the room, but now the blood was starting to seep through his clothes to form a wet, black stain. He tossed back a swallow of whiskey from the bottle he'd bought when he was on the trail and hissed as the fiery liquid coursed through his injured body.

George Rainer sat with his back in the corner of the room, giving him a view of the window and door simultaneously. The rifle was in his hands, but he'd removed the scope. The way he felt, he wouldn't need any help picking out his targets; just as he wouldn't be able to relax long enough to get any sleep.

"This is one helluva town," Scotelli mused as he held the bottle to his lips. "If we weren't on a job, I'd say we should stay for a while."

"This isn't a job, Pete. This is a whole mess of trouble that should have never happened."

Scotelli shrugged. "It happens. Sooner or later these rich bastards think they're too good to pay and need to be taught a lesson. If it weren't for that fella in Ulrich's office, I bet we'd have our money by now. That one's our problem."

Just then, a knock came on the door and Rainer was instantly on his feet to answer it. He looked to his partner for guidance as to whether his answer should be spoken or shouted from the mouth of his rifle.

"Who the hell is it?" Scotelli bellowed.

The answer was short, but more than either could have hoped for.

"Styles."

After a quick nod from Scotelli, Rainer lowered his rifle and stepped over to open the door. Standing outside, looking every bit as relaxed and in control as he usually did, was the man that had gotten both gunmen into the predicament they had so recently found themselves. Rainer took hold of the businessman by the lapel of his jacket and pulled him inside, all but tossing him into a rickety chair.

Although most of his calm had come from inside the bottle he was holding, Scotelli scooted forward until he was sitting on the edge of the bed. The liquor fell to the floor with a loud thunk, and his hand came to a rest on top of his gun. "You got the next five seconds to talk your way out of this one before both of us spill what's in your head onto that wall," he said.

Styles used the first two of those seconds to smooth out the creases in his clothing. "One more job," Styles finally said. "Two thousand for each of you. Half now, the other half upon completion."

The sound of Rainer levering his rifle crackled within the room. "Why would we ever trust you again?"

"Simple," the businessman explained. "I'm offering myself as a hostage until you receive your payment."

TWENTY-THREE

By the time Clint made it back to his room at the Prairie Dog, the saloon was mostly empty except for those who were staying the night there. Without the sounds of the player piano, showgirls, and hollering drunks roaring through his ears, Clint actually started to feel his shoulders relax from where they'd been drawn up in tense bundles.

He entered through a side door that was answered by a sleepy-eyed man with rolled up shirtsleeves and bags under his eyes. After shutting the door behind him, the man picked up a broom that had been leaning against the wall and continued sweeping the floor.

The sun would be up in just a few hours, but Clint felt as though he hadn't closed his eyes in weeks. His mind was racing with names, places, stories, and faces, but the rest of him was too damn tired to bother with it all. Before he knew it, he was up in his room, and the worst part of the whole thing was that he still couldn't allow himself to collapse onto the large bed.

He sluggishly grabbed a change of clothes and a few other essentials and prepared himself to head back out. Although he'd heard the footsteps coming down the hall, he didn't have the energy to look toward them until they'd stopped at his door. Luckily, the person standing there wasn't about to kill him. Not yet, anyway.

"Where have you been?" Maddy asked.

Clint was too tired to beat around any bushes. "The Three Aces. I needed to check in with your competition."

Although her arms crossed in front of her, Maddy didn't seem particularly upset. "And I see you decided to come back here," she said, smiling. "I'm glad you did."

"Yeah, well, I'm headed back that way now. Just needed to come by here and pick up some things."

Now, she looked upset. "But why? Especially when you would miss my exclusive service where I tuck in my favorite guest in person." She moved up close to him, reaching out to trace her hands over his chest and down to his waist. That's when she noticed the gash in his neck. "You're hurt!"

"I'll live."

She inspected the stitches and leaned in to kiss them gently. Satisfied that he'd been taken care of properly, she started kissing him more passionately. "I haven't ever had anything half as good as we had earlier. I don't know about you, but I was looking forward to another helping. That is . . . if you feel up to it."

Even through the fatigue and the pain, Clint felt the pleasure of her touch and his body responded in kind. Instinctively he rested a hand on the gentle slope of her hip and breathed in the spicy scent of her hair. "Miss Ulrich told me a lot of things, Maddy. Mainly about how you two have been fighting over territory when the whole country is wide open and waiting for saloons like this."

"Did she also tell you about the killers she sent to try and run me out of town?"

"What?"

Her hands held him more for security than anything else when she said those words. "That's right. Sent some crazies in here, offering to buy me out, and when I refused, they started trouble."

"Did they set any fires?"

Slowly she nodded, as though the memory of the whole thing pained her. "I don't think they wanted to burn the place down. Property's too valuable. But they did start a fire upstairs . . . down the hall from here, closer to my room. I think they wanted to kill me without hurting my place."

Clint held Maddy tightly when her body started to tremble. "Show me."

She took him by the hand and led him down the hall. There were a few others stumbling from room to room in various stages of consciousness. Unlike most hotels in the predawn hours, however, these stragglers were just finding their way into their rooms instead of heading out.

Maddy led him to the end of the narrow hall, past a dozen rooms, until they reached a set of double doors with PRIVATE painted across the middle. Even before they opened them, Clint could tell it was Maddy's room. The smell of her perfume and natural scent drifted from between the doors like a subtle beacon.

She opened them with a key that hung from a ribbon around her neck, reminding Clint of a child that was prone to losing things.

"Not a lot of pockets in what I usually wear," she said by way of explanation.

The inside of her room looked like two of the hotel suites had had their connecting wall knocked down and replaced with a bed that made the one in Clint's room look like bales of hay beneath a horse blanket in comparison. There was a small writing desk in one corner and a large picture window overlooking the intersection of Third and Carver. When things started opening again in a few hours, that intersection would be teeming with life.

"This doesn't look too damaged to me," Clint said.

Maddy closed the door and locked it. "I sleep here. You think I'd just leave all the smelly timber and burnt ashes behind for me to see when I wake up every morning?" Crossing the room in a bustle of dark hair and silk, Maddy stood near the window and pointed to the outer wall. "This is where it happened."

Clint walked over and took a closer look. He didn't have to be a carpenter to notice the section of newer wood that had replaced a portion of the wall roughly the size of a man crouching in the corner. "You say the men working for Miss Ulrich were responsible for this?"

"Not just me. Why don't you ask her yourself? She'll tell you just like she told me."

"She told you she ordered this?"

Nodding, Maddy gathered her skirts around her and sat down on the edge of her bed. "She told me the men she'd hired did it, but that she didn't order it."

"Do you believe her?"

"Enough to keep from turning her in to the sheriff. I suppose she also told you about the men I'd hired?"

Suddenly, Clint was feeling even more tired. "Yes, and to tell you the truth, I've heard so much today that my ears are about to close up on me."

"Then I won't bore you with another story. Let's just say that me and Miss Ulrich have a lot in common. We fight so harshly because we're so similar. We have the same good business sense," she said while gesturing to the saloon all around her. "The same good taste in fashion." Now her hands ran lightly over her cinched-in bosom and down to her shapely thighs. "Even the same taste in men."

"So is this all you wanted to show me?" Clint asked while pointing to the repaired wall. "Because the sooner I get moving, the sooner I can go to sleep."

"Can I ask you a question now?" Reaching out, Maddy snagged Clint by the wrist and pulled him down to the bed on top of her. "You've been getting to know me pretty well, Clint. Do you think I'm a killer?"

"That's not the point."

"All right. Then how about this. If either Greta or I wanted the other out of the saloon business that bad, don't you think at least one of these big ol' places would be burnt to the ground by now?"

Clint started to say something, but stopped himself. She definitely had a point and in his haste to try and see every angle, he'd almost overlooked the most obvious of facts.

"You get going, now," she said while pushing him back onto his feet. "And you think about who would gain the most from all that's happened. As for your sleeping arrangements—" shoving him out of her room, Maddy turned to the side and let her dress fall to the floor, exposing her naked, supple body in a breathtaking silhouette. "—I'm sure you'll make the right decision."

Then the door shut in Clint's face.

TWENTY-FOUR

Clint staggered back into the Three Aces as the first hint of dawn was breaking across the sky. It wasn't much in the autumn morning, but the slight shift in light was enough to make Clint feel more tired than he'd been in a long while. In all honesty, he had no idea how late it was or, more accurately for this time of day, how early. All he knew was that he needed to get some sleep if he was going to be much good to anyone anytime soon.

Unlike the Prairie Dog, the Three Aces would close for an hour to get the big cleaning jobs done. They were just opening again when Clint came back and the smell of breakfast was thick in the air. There was bacon, eggs, steak, potatoes, and fresh corn bread, but none of it kept him from dragging himself upstairs and into his room.

The instant his head hit the pillow, he was dead to the world. He never even got out of his boots.

When he awoke, Clint was under the covers. At first, he didn't think much of it, but then he realized somebody was in the room with him. His eyes shot open and blood surged through his system, causing him to sit bolt upright in his bed. He'd left his gun on the bedpost, and he started to reach for it.

Standing at the window, Greta Ulrich nearly jumped off the floor at the suddenness of Clint's movement.

"Oh, good lord!" she yelped in shock. Greta put a hand over her chest and started laughing nervously once she saw what it was that had startled her so. "I thought you were going to sleep the whole day away, Clint. How are you feeling?"

Clint rubbed his eyes as the momentary rush of energy left him dreary and dazed. "Like I could sleep the rest of the day away. What time is it?"

"Just past eleven."

"What are you doing in my room?"

"I came to check on you and found you sprawled out in a heap on the bed, so I tucked you up."

That bothered Clint. She should never have been able to do that without waking him. Was he finally getting so old his instincts were going?

Greta turned to face him and walked toward the bed. She looked like a different woman from the night before, dressed in a simple white dress that was tied at the waist and loose around the neckline. Her fine, rounded breasts swayed back and forth with every step. The closer she got, the harder her nipples seemed to become.

She took her time walking across the room, and when she finally reached his side, she sat next to him and leaned down to whisper in his ear, letting her dress fall away to reveal the supple curves beneath.

"I told you last night," she said in a soft, throaty voice. "I need to thank you properly for saving my life."

Clint started to say something, but was stopped by a gentle brush of her fingertips against his lips. Greta made a soft shushing sound as she reached up to loosen the leather tie that held her hair neatly in place, and as it came loose, it fell down her back, spilling over her shoulders and drifting lazily in front of her eyes.

Next, she pulled at a string that laced the front of her dress together. Her breasts pushed apart the material that had previously been binding. Dark nipples hardened even further when he looked at them, as if she could feel the touch of his glance upon her body.

Slowly she peeled back the blankets and sensuously began to remove his clothes, right down to his boots and underwear. He enjoyed the motion of her body as she allowed her dress to fall away even more, and her breasts swung free of the material completely.

"Greta, you don't have to," Clint started to say before he felt her touch once again on his mouth.

"I know, Clint." Pulling the dress down over her waist, she lifted one knee and then another until she'd crawled out of her clothing and kicked it onto the floor. "But I want to."

Clint's cock was stiff and exposed between his legs. She looked down at it hungrily while cupping it gently in her hands. Her fingers went to work, delicately caressing his shaft until it ached for satisfaction.

Overcome by the sheer pleasure of her touch, Clint leaned back and pushed his head back into his pillow. Greta shook her hair out so that it draped down and brushed against Clint's skin as she moved down along his chest and stomach. She stopped when her face was directly over Clint's pole and licked her lips. Her eyes darted over to find that he was staring anxiously back at her, waiting for her to satisfy his growing need.

She moved even more slowly toward his member. When she got close enough, he could feel her hot breath on his cock. With a sudden, flicking motion, her tongue slipped out to moisten its swollen head. Then she pursed her lips together . . . and blew.

The feel of her breath on him, combined with the sudden change from hot to cold, made Clint shudder. A wave of sensation jumped from his groin all the way up along his spine and back again. It took every ounce of his strength to keep from grabbing hold of Greta and taking her. Clint knew such a move would be more than welcomed, but he wanted to see just how good she could make him feel.

Greta was smiling at him when she saw his reaction. "You like that?" she whispered.

Before Clint could answer, she had him in her mouth. Her lips pressed tight against his shaft as her head moved down along its length. When she got to its base, she stopped and clenched her throat around him, squeezing him gently until he was about to explode.

As if sensing every mood of his body, she eased up and raised her head. Her lips parted in a wide smile, exposing clean white teeth as they ran gently along his member. With the tip still in her mouth, Greta looked up and stared wantonly into Clint's eyes, knowing full well what he wanted to do next.

Her hands reached up to massage his stomach and knead the muscles in his chest, holding him down just as he started to sit up and reach toward her. Once again, her lips closed around him. They looked like red bows and felt warm and wet as she sucked him, her head bobbing up and down, faster and faster.

The noise she made sounded like she was savoring a ripe peach, and when she swallowed, it was loud enough for him to hear. He thought he couldn't get any harder, then she reached down to gently stroke the tender area beneath his shaft, which made him lean straight back again with his eyes rolling in his head.

Clint reached forward to run his fingers through the silken strands of her hair. When he put his hand on the back of her head, he heard Greta moan with pleasure. The sound she made caused a vibration in her throat that was almost too much for Clint to bear.

Sensing the height of pleasure she'd taken him to, Greta eased up on her attentions and slipped him from her mouth. "You taste so good," she purred. "I want to taste it all." Then she shifted her body around until she sat astride Clint's face, holding her moist pussy just above his mouth as she said, "I want you to taste it all, too."

In response, Clint lifted his mouth to the thatch of blond hair between her finely toned legs and ran his tongue from the little pink nub at the top all the way down the length of her thin, trembling lips.

Greta arched her back as the pleasure raked along every nerve. When he had his tongue probing hungrily inside of her, she bent down and devoured him as if he were her last meal.

Clint reached up to cup her tight backside in his hands, pushing her closer so he could bury his face between her thighs. She returned the favor and, finally, both of their bodies started to shake. Each of their moans were muffled by the other's body, and when they couldn't stand any more, they cried out as the pleasure shook them to their cores.

Greta swallowed every drop of him and licked him clean.

With her legs clamped around the sides of his head, Clint could feel her becoming wetter and hotter. He drank down her juices as if they were honey, and after she finally climbed off of him, he was afraid he actually might sleep through the day completely.

TWENTY-FIVE

Scotelli had been more than happy to oblige Styles in his request. Taking the businessman hostage wasn't quite on the top of his list of things to do to the man who'd shortchanged him, but it was damn close to it. One of the things that had been higher up on his priorities was putting a bullet through his skull. Instead, Scotelli had to be satisfied with spending the previous night beating him to within an inch of his life.

When the sun came up, it shone through the frilly curtains that had been made by the shaky hands of the old woman who owned the boardinghouse. The light glanced off the top of a bowl of water kept on a stand near the bed, across the room, and onto the face of Kenneth Styles.

Where the well-dressed man had used to look refined and collected, he now had a desperate wildness in his eyes similar to a goat staked out for the lions. In the back of his mind, he tried to hold on to the notion that his plan was sound, but the pain that ravaged most of his body was begging to differ. He'd passed out last night after Scotelli had grown too tired to keep hitting him and woke up this morning to a splash of warm water across his face.

"Rise and shine, shit head," Scotelli leered as he set a tin mug on the floor. "You ready to start explaining yourself?"

Originally, Styles had planned on talking his way out of any possible harm the minute he got the hired guns to put down their weapons the night before. But the Italian had other notions. Unfortunately for Styles, he couldn't do much fast-talking with a gag buried so far down his throat that he was on the verge of puking all night long.

When the gag was finally pulled from his mouth, Styles felt as if his tongue was being yanked from his head. The gag had bruised him from the inside out, and when it finally came loose, he vomited uncontrollably all over his precious suit.

Scotelli thought that was the funniest thing he'd ever seen. "Aw, Jesus," he said through teary-eyed laughter. "Now that's actually worth the trouble of cleaning up. Would ya look at that, George?"

Rainer, who'd just returned, was tired of seeing the other man suffer. Every day, he grew more certain that his partner's temper would get them captured and probably killed. "I see it," Rainer said. "Now would you keep him quiet before that old lady comes up here?"

As if in response to the words, a knock came on the door.

"Is everything all right in there, boys?" came the wavering voice of the boardinghouse owner. "Do you have a guest in there with you?"

"Yes, ma'am," Scotelli chimed innocently. "He won't want any breakfast, but we'll be down shortly."

There was a pause and a nervous shuffling of feet, but then the footsteps started moving back toward the staircase. "If he wants to stay, it'll be extra," she hollered over her shoulder.

Scotelli glared with a murderous grin directly into Styles's face, clamping a hand over the businessman's mouth. "Oh, yes, ma'am!"

After the footsteps had clomped down the stairs, Scotelli moved his hand away from Styles and wagged his finger in front of him. "Now don't make me get in trouble by making any more noise. Especially if I have to shoot you. That's awful loud."

Styles began to talk, but the words caught painfully in the back of his parched throat. "You . . . you haven't heard my proposition."

"We ain't listening to another word that comes from your lying mouth," Rainer said while checking out the window to watch the activity on the street. There wasn't much to see, but even at this early hour there were plenty of folks starting their day.

The boardinghouse was near a stretch of stores and bakeries, giving the air the pleasant smell of a giant kitchen. Every breeze that came through the open window was cool and rich with the scents of warm bread. Farther inside the room, closer to Styles, the air was stifling. It stunk of blood, fear, and now vomit.

The businessman couldn't be further out of his element. All his self-control was gone. Every bit of calm had been replaced by pain and panic. "Then let me go," he pleaded. "If you don't want to be rich, then let me go, and we'll forget any of this ever happened."

Scotelli, who'd been lifting his nose to the delicious flavor of the wind, turned suddenly on the man tied to the chair and sent a vicious backhand across his mouth. The blow reopened a deep gash that had just begun to scab over.

"For a schooled man, you're pretty damn stupid," Scotelli said. "You've been sittin' there in your own blood all night so you would never forget about what happened. You cheat me again, and you'll be sitting in a chair just like that one for as long as I can keep you alive. When you do die, it'll be as slow and painful as I can make it."

"Now," Scotelli said once the businessman had had a chance to pull himself together, "let's hear about this deal of yours."

TWENTY-SIX

Clint woke up after another much-deserved hour of sleep. He dressed and made his way downstairs to find that business in the saloon was well under way. The crowd wasn't as large as it would get later in the evening, but there was a fair amount of people scattered throughout the place. Only at this time, they were more at the dining and gambling tables than at the bar.

Taking a quick walk through the Three Aces' main room, Clint looked for any trace of Kenneth Styles. He could find no sign of him, so he settled in to order a late breakfast.

When he was halfway through a plate of fried potatoes, bacon, and toast, Clint saw Greta Ulrich heading his way. She sat down and gave him a naughty little smile.

"Is everything to your satisfaction?" she asked.

"Yes, my accommodations have been quite fine, thank you."

"I'd join you for some of that, but I just ate."

Clint couldn't help but laugh.

Regaining her composure, Greta moved her chair so that she was sitting closer to his side. "Someone's been asking to talk to you," she said.

"Styles?"

"No. Actually, I've been asking around about him and nobody's seen him since last night. It's the sheriff who's looking for you. It's about last night."

"Well, I can think of a few questions for him, myself. Where is he?"

"Over there," she said, indicating the end of the bar closest to the front door.

The man she pointed to was short and balding. There weren't many people between them, allowing Clint to get a good look at the other man. The sheriff stood with one hand on the bar and the other on his knee. He had the shape of an over-ripe pear and wore his gun in a shoulder rig on top of a dirty tan shirt. What little hair he had was in a ring around his scalp and looked more maintained than most women's. As if sensing Clint's examination, the sheriff turned toward him and gave a single wave.

Clint picked up his last piece of toast and his cup of coffee before standing. "What's his name?" he asked.

"Sheriff Cole."

"Let's hope I'm not in too much trouble."

Watching Clint walk around the table, Greta said under her breath, "He should be the one thanking you for taking care of things last night when he was too slow to get here himself."

Making a straight line across the saloon, Clint set his coffee onto the bar and popped the last bite of toast into his mouth.

"You'd be Mister Clint Adams?" the sheriff asked.

"Yes, I would." Clint extended his hand. "So that would make you Sheriff Cole."

The sheriff's grip was soft and clammy, but his smile seemed genuine enough. "I've got to admit that I've heard of you, Mister Adams. That is . . . if you're *the* Clint Adams."

Some times more that others, Clint wished he could just be another anonymous face instead of having his reputation always hanging around him like a sign on his chest.

"I'm that one all right," Clint said. "Miss Ulrich said you wanted to speak to me?"

Cole grimaced as though he'd spoken out of turn. "I hate to bother you, but I do need you to come down to my office for a bit to answer some questions."

"Can't you ask them here?"

"Yes, but . . ."

Clint had every respect for the law, but he didn't much care for lawmen who acted like they would rather be storekeepers.

Men like that didn't even try to show any strength when doing their jobs, which had led to dangerous circumstances more times than Clint could count. Cole was one of those men, and he seemed too fidgety to command any respect. Too soft to uphold the law.

"The questions I need to ask are regarding the, uh, gunplay last night," Cole continued uncomfortably. "I know it wasn't much for someone like you, but we don't get a lot of violence in Mandrake."

"I understand, Sheriff, but I'd be willing to answer all your questions here. It would save us the walk."

"Actually, there was something else."

Clint nodded. "That's what I thought."

"Uh, I'm going to have to ask you for your, uh, gun."

"Nobody was killed, Sheriff. All that happened was that someone lost their temper and shot up Miss Ulrich's office. Since she doesn't want to press charges on that or against me, I'd say there's no reason for you to take my gun. I might need it if that man comes looking for me."

"Which is exactly what I'm afraid of. We get a lot of types in this town. Drunks and gamblers mostly, drawn to our night-life, but not a lot of killers."

"That surprises me. Usually the drunks and gamblers I run into tend to have done their share of killing as well."

"Not in Mandrake," Cole said. "Not just yet."

"Shouldn't you be looking for the man responsible for last night's shooting?"

"I don't suppose you know who it was?"

"Well, I do know he worked for a man I saw in town myself last night."

"You know where I might find him?"

"Maybe we can look together," Clint said as he sipped his coffee. "I've got some things of my own I need to ask him. The funny thing is, even though he wears the suit and talks like an uptown banker, this man I'm thinking of is responsible for burning down an entire town. And the man working for him came in here, drew down on me, and nearly killed several people in this saloon. He had another man with him with a rifle. If anyone had made a move in the wrong direction, that one would have put him down in a flash."

Shifting on his feet, Sheriff Cole ran the palm of his hand over the smooth skin on top of his head. "I don't see what any of that has to do with—"

"It has plenty to do with what you're talking about, Sheriff. Because, even with all those types of men running loose in your town, you decided to come over here and ask me for my gun. Hell, me and the bouncers in this place were the only ones who did anything when the lead started to fly. I never saw you till just now. Didn't anyone call you last night?"

Sheriff Cole started to answer, but was too flustered to finish a sentence. Finally, he reached toward the bar and grabbed hold of a new Stetson hat that had been taking up space in front of him. After plopping it onto his head, he hooked both thumbs through his belt and puffed his chest.

"I heard you were a reasonable man, Mister Adams. A man that respected the law. You keep your gun, but you better watch your step. If you don't want to help me, then that's all well and good. If I hear about you drawing that gun and shooting up any part of my town, I'll come back for you, Gunsmith or not."

Finally the sheriff had earned the first bit of respect in Clint's mind.

"And what about those others I told you about?" Clint asked.

"I'll find them and Styles in my own time . . . and without your help. But if they shoot at anyone else, it's on your head for not helping me when you had the chance."

His point made, the sheriff turned and waddled out the door.

Funny, but Clint had never mentioned Styles's name to the sheriff. He thought that over while signaling for a second cup of coffee.

TWENTY-SEVEN

After giving the sheriff enough time to get back to the comfort of his office, Clint decided to start looking for Styles on his own. He began by trying to find the dealer who'd been at the table where he and Styles had played their game of poker. It was too early for the dealer to be working, but Clint was able to put enough cash in front of the man who was at the table to find out where he should look.

"That'd be Bill," the dealer said after agreeing upon a price for the information. "He comes on after four every evenin', but you should be able to find him home until then." He gave Clint an address on Fifth Street.

Clint took the walk and found Bill, but didn't get much that was of any help. All the dealer had to say was that the banker had been at his table for a few hours before Clint got there and they'd left together. Once the shooting had started, he'd lost track of the man in all the confusion.

Hardly worth the price Clint had paid to find the dealer's house.

Although it was nice to be in the fresh air and open space, Clint decided to head back toward the Prairie Dog to check and see if Styles had made his way over there. When he entered the saloon on Third Street, Clint saw he was starting to be recognized by the workers as one of their frequent customers. It was an honor shared by several of the unshaven men asleep with their heads on a table and a bottle at their feet. Even so, it made the people in the white aprons a little more affable and ready to talk.

Clint ordered a beer and left enough money on the bar for three or four more.

"You need something else?" the bartender asked while eyeing the money.

"Just some information. Have you seen a man in here in a fancy suit, probably saying he was a banker?" Clint went on to describe Styles to the young man, who had to lean forward to catch every word that was said.

"He sounds rich. We get a lot of people through here, but most of the rich ones tend to head for the Three Aces. Did you check there?"

"Yes, but this man might have been here a few times. Were you working here when they had the fire?"

The bartender's face dropped, and he nodded solemnly. "I remember that all right. We thought the place was set to burn down what with all the smoke and all. Started upstairs if I recall. Nearly killed Maddy and some of the guests in their rooms." Suddenly, he stopped and rubbed his chin.

"Y'know what?" the bartender mused. "Seems I remember a man like you described hanging around here an awful lot right before the fire. Probably not the fella you're after, but he was coming in all the time, askin' to talk to Maddy."

"Did she do business with him?"

"Not unless she tosses all her partners out on their ear into the street!" Laughing at his own joke, the barkeep slapped the well-polished wood that they were both leaning against. "Nah, I don't think Maddy was too fond of that one."

"Where did he like to stay when he was in town? Here, at the Prairie Dog?"

The bartender pondered that one long enough to be called away by a customer. After a fair amount of socializing with an old man who liked to take his brandy before lunch, the young man in the apron returned. His expression was the same as a dog who was overly proud of the dead pheasant in its mouth.

"I remember now," he said as Clint was getting up to leave.

"Better than that, I remember seeing that fella just the other night."

"He was here?"

"Yeah, but not for too long. Stopped in to ask for Maddy, but she wasn't here. Then he moved on and said he had some business to take care of with Miss Ulrich."

It wasn't much, but at least it was something.

"Thanks," Clint said. And then he turned again toward the door.

"Wait! There's something else."

"I'm listening."

"I heard someone mention a banker earlier today. Maddy got a message from him about an hour ago. One of the girls that keeps an eye on Maddy's affairs was lookin' for her to give her the message, and I caught the name. Styles, wasn't it?"

Clint nodded. "Any chance you could find out what that message said?"

"Maybe . . ." The bartender made an awkward try for subtlety as he slid his hand over the bar, palm up, toward Clint.

Clint put a few coins in his hand and then snatched them out again before the bartender could make a fist. "If you're thinking of making something up," Clint warned, "I'd suggest you try and come up with a way to spend your money real quick, because you won't have much time before I catch up to you."

"I may not get all the words right, but I can remember what it was about. Besides, you can always ask Claire. She'll remember if you need to know everything exact."

Clint dropped the coins back into the barkeep's hand and left them there.

"It mentioned another payment that was due and that it needed to be there by ten tonight. But the strange thing is that it was addressed to Maddy *and* Miss Ulrich."

"Both of them owe a payment?"

"Looks that way."

"Payment for what?"

"I don't get my nose too far into my employer's affairs. Not far enough to get caught, anyway."

"Did you catch any mention of where the payment was supposed to be delivered?" Clint asked.

"No. All I remember is what I told you."

Suddenly, Clint came up with the next place he needed to go and nearly kicked himself for not thinking of it sooner. "Thanks for all your help," he said to the bartender. "And if anyone asks about me . . . what do you know?"

"Not a damn thing, Mister Adams." The bartender found enough of his courage to put his hand back out onto the bar. "Not even your name."

Clint couldn't help but admire the barkeep's guts, if not his common sense. Still, he flipped a half dollar into the waiting palm, which snapped around it fast enough to make a clapping sound.

When Clint left the Prairie Dog, he turned off of Third Street and kept walking through the shopping district. An entire street lined with butchers, grocers, and bakers who gave the air an edible flavor that was far enough removed from the smoky odor of the saloons that Clint felt as though he were in a different town. It was a part of Mandrake that had been dark and empty when he'd first arrived, and Clint promised himself to return when he had enough time to sample some of the goods he was smelling.

For the moment, however, he was heading toward a whole other set of smells that wouldn't be half as pleasant as the ones he was leaving behind. Hopefully, Arlen would have something to say that would make Clint's trip to the livery worth his while.

TWENTY-EIGHT

As always, Arlen was easy to find, sitting outside his stables in an old chair that seemed just strong enough to support his weight. When Clint approached, the liveryman was leaning back against the old barn with his legs crossed, whittling on a piece of fresh hickory.

He was whistling softly to himself until Clint got close enough to get hit by a stray sliver of wood as it flew from the stick in his hand.

"Mornin'," Arlen said with a tip of his floppy farmer's hat. "Come to check on yer horse? He's a beaut."

Clint leaned against the barn next to Arlen's chair, looking from side to side to check if there was anyone else about. There wasn't. "That and to talk for a while."

Arlen stopped whittling and leaned forward until the front two legs of his chair touched the soil. "You don't strike me as the sociable type. You got somethin' specific you wanted to talk about?"

"Did you hear the shooting last night?"

Nodding, Arlen looked down at the gun at Clint's side. "That was you, I suppose?"

"I was more on the receiving end."

"That ain't what I heard. Way I heard it was that you was the only one that hit much of anything besides the walls." Laughing, Arlen added, " 'Course, with all the drinkin' that goes on in this town, that ain't much of a surprise."

"You see a lot, don't you, Arlen?"

"I try to be in the right place at the right time."

"Then maybe you can help me. I need to know where I can find the men that did the shooting last night. I'm pretty sure they'd be new in town, and I figure they might have stopped by here to put their horses up. Maybe they left word as far as where they were headed."

"First one came in late last night. He was all fired up about something and damn near rode his horse into the ground getting himself here. I'm lucky to be feeding that mare rather than burying it. Second one came in a few hours later. That fella seemed dangerous, but not crazy, you know?"

Clint nodded.

"That second one asked for the name of a good boardinghouse in town since he didn't want to stay in no saloon. I gave him a place over on Bond Street, not too far from here, where all the bakers and meat cutters set up shop."

Even at the mention of it, Clint could once again smell the mouthwatering aromas of his walk through that part of town. "I know it," he said.

"That's where I steered 'em, but who's to say if they decided to go there or not."

"Do you know if they're still in town?"

"Well, if they aren't, they both left their horses behind," Arlen said while hitching a thumb over his shoulder to indicate a pair of animals sharing one of the larger stalls. "Like I said, the first one didn't care a bit for his. Told me I could keep it if it survived the night. But that second one . . . he was concerned enough to ease up on the ride into town. My guess is he'd be back for her before he left."

"Thanks, Arlen. I knew you'd have your eyes open." Picking out enough to cover half a week's stay for Eclipse, Clint dropped the sum into the top pocket of Arlen's coveralls. "That's to cover my own expenses for the past day. Keep the change."

"Normally, I'd say no to such a generous offer, but I'd hate to do something like that in the face of such a kind act. I don't suppose I could impose on you further?"

"That depends on what your favor is."

"Just to send one of the boys from the Prairie Dog down here with a fresh bottle for me. Tonight looks to be a real mess of cold for my old bones."

The air actually felt like it was warming up to Clint, but he had better things to do now than debate the weather. If it wasn't for Arlen, however, Clint wouldn't have had much of anything to do that would have been half as productive. "I'll have someone bring it over tonight. Now, I'm going to go check on my horse before you decide to fleece me for anything else."

"Don't you worry," Arlen said with a tip of his hat as he went back to his whittling. "I'm all through fleecing for today."

Despite the fact that Clint never actually saw Arlen inside the barn doing any work, Eclipse seemed to be in fine shape. Clint held his hand up to the horse's nose and then scratched him behind the ears. Eclipse seemed anxious, but not overly so.

There was a sound coming from the other end of the stalls. It was more than just footsteps. They were footsteps taken with a purpose. That wasn't enough to put Clint completely on his guard, but the sound of a gun being slowly drawn from its holster . . . that was more than enough.

Clint's hand flashed to his weapon, but held fast as soon as he heard a hammer being clicked into firing position.

"I got tired of waiting for ya," came a voice from within the shadows of the barn's far corner. "Drop that gun belt to the floor."

Clint recognized the voice from Edgar's saloon. He could picture the gangly little man as he unbuckled his holster and let it fall. Behind him, Red's heart was pounding, and he stared at a spot between Clint's shoulders with the dark, sunken eyes of a desperate man. The smell of whiskey hung around him like a bitter cloud.

"Let me guess," Clint said while glancing over his shoulder. "You're here to collect your payment, too."

Red wasn't the kind of man to travel alone, so Clint was already on the alert for someone else sneaking up on him. As far as he could tell, however, the only people in the old barn were himself and the spindly runt behind him, who still sounded a little scared even though he was the only one heeled.

Red moved so he was positioned far enough away to keep out of arm's reach, but close enough to give himself an easy shot. "Maybe I'm here to kill you," Red sneered. "That's more'n enough reason."

"Sure, but that would mean you knew who I was back in Wayne and followed me all the way here, keeping yourself hidden until this very moment. You're not that smart."

Red's nostrils flared, which almost looked comical on such a slight man. He held the gun in front of him, leveling it at Clint's head. "I could'a shot you, when . . ." Trailing off, he caught himself right before telling Clint about the room he'd secured next to his at the Prairie Dog. Then he shook his head smugly. "But that don't matter 'cause I can kill you right now."

"Is that all you want?" Clint asked. "To be the man who kills me . . . like this?"

"I'll be famous. Then rich."

"You'll be remembered like Bob Ford. A pathetic little man who shot a famous one in the back. If he'd killed Jesse in a fair fight, that might have been different."

Red's finger was tensing on the trigger, making the barrel of his gun waver slightly in Clint's face. One twitch was all he needed. "You sayin' you want a fair fight?"

"No. I want to handle my business here and leave. But if you want fame, you won't get it this way."

He thought it over and made his decision, a thin smile sneaking over ratlike features. "I'll take my chances with fame," Red said, "but not with you."

Clint knew he had less than a second to dodge a bullet.

TWENTY-NINE

Clint's muscles snapped into action like coiled springs. In one swift motion, he'd dropped to one knee and drawn his gun, just as Red's first shot exploded over his head. Clint could feel the bullet cut through the air above him just as he could feel the speed in the other man that was one part crazy and another part fear.

Firing from the hip, Clint got off a shot that clipped Red's side as the other man threw himself toward one of the nearby open stalls.

The lead burned a painful trail through Red's flesh, cutting him open between two of his ribs. He scrambled to get his feet beneath him and line up his next shot, but Clint was too fast. As soon as he'd worked himself into a low squatting position, Red heard another set of explosions as wood splinters rained down on top of his head. Looking up, he saw two fresh holes had been blown through the thin wall separating his stall from the next.

Clint was still on one knee as he fired through the flimsy wall that Red had chosen as his cover. While heading for a stack of hay of bales in a crouching run, he looked behind him to check the large front door. From what he could see, Arlen was just standing there watching. Clint wasn't sure if he had a rifle in his hands.

Clint pitched himself facedown to the straw-covered floor

when he realized the man at the door was way too skinny to be Arlen. Just as he'd figured, Red was not the kind of man to work alone.

The rifle cracked a split-second before Clint's face slammed against the dirty wooden planks, sending a slug into the bales. Another shot echoed loudly in the barn, which was soon followed by a heavy thundering noise that sounded like a wild horse's hooves pounding on the floor behind him.

Unfortunately, that was exactly what it was.

While a few of the animals being kept in the livery were used to gunfire, the one in Clint's stall was spooked to the point of bucking against the leather straps tying it in place. Clint was hiding in a closet-sized compartment formed by the hay bales on one side and a water trough on the other. When Clint realized where the closest horse was, its powerful hind legs had already smashed through the trough as if it hadn't even been there.

"Close him in!" Red yelled to the man with the rifle.

Clutching his free hand to his bloody ribs, Red propped himself up against a wall and used his legs to push himself back up onto his feet. His breath was ragged, and his heart pounded in his chest. He couldn't believe it, but not only had he found The Gunsmith, he also had him cornered. Peeking over the dividing wall, he looked toward his partner.

The rifleman looked down the long barrel and sighted out his next shot. There was another crack, a puff of smoke, and the snap of brittle wood being chipped apart by flying lead.

Clint pressed himself as tightly as he could against the ground as the rifle's bullet passed through the trough and started a little stream of water, emptying directly onto his forehead. He was in a crossfire, which meant that neither one of the other men had to be particularly good with their weapons to put him in a world of hurt. He waited for the sound of the rifle being cocked, and when he heard it, he launched himself into a forward roll, landing in a low crouch in the middle of the barn's open space.

Red was watching intently, hoping for his shot. The moment he saw movement coming from where Clint was hiding, he stepped out and thumbed back his hammer.

The rifleman also chose this moment to close in and quickly

adjusted his aim when he saw his target burst from behind the now-empty trough.

Clint waited a second until his gut, more than anything else, told him to fire. His body swiveled, and he concentrated on a specific target. Squeezing the trigger while starting his next roll, Clint didn't wait to see the results of his shot before getting himself out of the open.

Clint's round cut through the air before chewing into the rifleman's fingers, severing two of them completely before knocking the rifle barrel up just as it was fired. The man behind the rifle hollered like a stuck pig as the fingers that had been wrapped below the barrel dropped to the floor. His other hand had already pulled back the trigger, which sent his shot off target and into Red's stomach.

All Red could make out was a blur of motion and two separate muzzle flashes. Before he could draw a bead on Clint, he felt something punch into his gut, doubling him over as white-hot fingers of pain lanced through his entire body.

By the time Clint had rolled to the opposite side of the barn, he could still hear the gunshots going off around him. Since he wasn't hit, he knew his bullet had found its mark. As for the rest, it had been a gamble. Judging by the painful cries coming from Red, that gamble had also paid off.

The gunfire stopped as quickly as it had started. Other sounds quickly followed, but were much more welcome to Clint's ears. First, there was the solid thud of a body hitting the floor. Then came a heavy clatter as the rifleman let the weapon slip from his disfigured hand.

Clint found himself in another stall. Only this time, he'd looked before his leap and wound up crouched down next to Eclipse. At least he wasn't in any danger of getting his head knocked off. Reaching up to put a hand on the horse's flank, Clint moved the stallion back to clear the line of fire.

He waited for a few seconds, but could only hear the sounds of wounded men as the pain started playing hell with their bodies and minds. Carefully, he eased from the stall and took a look around.

Red had dropped to a sitting position on the floor. He'd managed to push himself back against a post for support, but the wound in his stomach had already turned his shirt black from blood. His sunken eyes darted from side to side without really seeing much, and his gun lay forgotten by his side.

As for the rifleman, Clint recognized his face as soon as the other man stumbled into a shaft of light. He'd seen that one in Edgar's saloon. It was one of the others who'd been sitting at Red's table that day, which now seemed so long ago. He was too busy staring at the bloody stubs that had once been the fingers of his left hand to notice Clint's approach.

"Drop it," Clint said while raising his pistol to cover the rifleman.

The man was still too stunned to listen, so Clint stepped over and snatched the rifle from his hand. The stock was slippery with blood, so Clint tossed it in the air and grabbed it on its way down, his hand wrapped around the grip and his finger on the trigger.

"Go sit next to your friend over there."

Two guns pointing at him were more than enough to get the man's attention, and he stumbled over to where Red was sitting. He was still holding his wounded hand up to his face when he dropped roughly onto his seat.

These two had managed to get the drop on him, which didn't sit well at all with Clint. When he'd heard the report of a rifle, he'd been expecting to see the man who'd covered Scotelli standing at the barn's door. Instead, Clint had found out the hard way that there were even more people after him than he had thought.

THIRTY

Arlen poked his head around the corner once he was certain the shooting had stopped. Seeing that Clint was the one standing, he walked into his old barn and took in the whole scene.

"What the blazes is goin' on in here?" he said while checking on the horses in the closest stalls.

Clint was collecting all the guns and piling them up next to Eclipse. "Call the sheriff and get a doctor in here quick. Get a rag or something to help that one," he said while pointing to Red. "He's been gut-shot."

"Aww hell," Arlen grumbled while he ran for a pile of cloths in the corner. "This is exactly why I'd rather spend my day with horses instead of the folks that ride 'em. They ain't nothin' but trouble."

Clint was about to reply, but spun around to face the door. He saw a figure running full-throttle toward the livery with gun in hand. The shape was plump and waddling with every step, a new Stetson sitting firmly in place.

"Nobody move!" Sheriff Cole shouted.

Arlen's hands shot into the air, while Clint held his casually out to the sides. The sheriff was trying not to look as out of breath as he felt, but was about as good an actor as he was a runner.

"I heard the shooting," Cole said. "Arlen, tell me what happened."

"He came to check on his horse," the liveryman said while pointing at Clint. "Next thing I know, I hear gunshots and that other fella came walking around from the side of my barn so he could get his shots in, too."

Sheriff Cole seemed very pleased with himself when he said, "Mister Adams, I'm now going to have to insist that you hand over your—"

"Son of a bitch!"

The shouted curse came from the other end of the barn. Clint, Arlen, and the sheriff all turned at once to get a look at who'd spoken, and they were all just in time to see the insane look on Red's face as he pulled a gun from his boot and aimed it at them.

A shot echoed through the barn and a third eye appeared on Red's forehead. His body seemed to shrink as the life drained out of him. Red's partner seemed to have been making his own move, but stopped short when he saw that Red had already been taken out.

Sheriff Cole stood rooted to the spot. Next to him, Clint stood tall and sure, his right hand extended and gripping the smoking pistol that had just ended Red's life. Clint walked forward to push the gun against the rifleman's skull.

"You have any more surprises, you'd better play them now," he said.

Red's partner was too scared to talk, so he shook his head instead.

"Didn't think so. Toss out any guns you've got."

He did as he was told, removing with shaky hands a two-shot Derringer from his sleeve.

"Now go over to the sheriff with your hands over your head," Clint commanded. "If I see you again, I'll put you in the ground right next to your partner."

The remaining man was stared into silence by Clint as he was searched thoroughly and had his hands tied behind his back.

"How about it, Sheriff?" Clint asked. "You still feel like taking my gun or should I check back with you after you clean this mess up?"

As much as Sheriff Cole wanted to follow through with his original course of action, he just couldn't get himself to do it.

"Seeing as how this was obviously a case of self-defense, I'll let you off with a warning. But that doesn't mean I want to see you standing over any more corpses. Do you understand me?"

"I was on my way out," Clint said as he turned to leave. Before he go too far away, he was stopped by the sheriff's grating voice.

"Adams!"

Clint stood and waited, but didn't turn around.

"Be careful," Cole said to his back.

"Always am." Then Clint was off, and he didn't stop until the smell of home cooking was once again in his nostrils.

George Rainer looked through the scope of his rifle, waiting for the man coming from the livery to walk within shooting range. He recognized that one as the man from the Three Aces, and Scotelli had pointed the man out as the one who'd faced him down.

Behind Rainer, still tied to the chair, was Kenneth Styles. The businessman had finally quieted down enough for Rainer to think straight. And somewhere down on the street was Scotelli. His partner had wanted to keep walking between the two saloons to see what happened once they got the letters Styles had told him to deliver.

Rainer didn't think for a moment that either one of the saloon owners would pay up and be done with it. Not without any proper convincing by way of lead or fire. They were no different than the others. Hopefully, Scotelli would be true to his word and put this town behind them once they got the pay they had coming. Rainer was tired of all this dealing with Styles, and he was tired of Mandrake. The longer he stayed in town, the more he thought they might not make it out alive.

Rainer was still sitting in front of the open window when he spotted the four men coming down the street. They were dressed in riding clothes and wool coats. Not too unusual for the crisp weather, but it wasn't the clothes that got under Rainer's skin. It was the way they walked.

They carried themselves with purpose and didn't waste a movement, not even to return the glances they were getting from the folks they passed. He watched those men closely until they walked straight up to the boardinghouse's front door. The first man pulled the door open and let the others walk inside. Before entering himself, he looked straight up at Rainer and locked him in place with a stare that was cold as death. After what felt like an eternity, the man picked up his pace and hurried inside.

Turning on Styles, Rainer cocked his rifle and trained it on the door.

"They're here, aren't they?" Styles asked through swollen lips.

Suddenly, Rainer knew what was happening. And with that realization came panic like he'd never felt before.

He began shooting through the door as soon as he heard the heavy footsteps pounding up the stairs. He kept firing as they echoed down the hall. In the time it took for him to lever in another round, the door was kicked in, giving him a glimpse of two of the men that he'd spotted on the street.

They ducked to either side when he fired at them, and when he worked the lever again, one of them appeared in the door frame.

The last thing Rainer saw was a cloud of smoke and the faces of those men. They were all in the room before he hit the ground. Once his ears stopped ringing and before the darkness overtook him, Rainer heard one of the men speak.

"Are you all right, Mister Styles?" the killer asked.

And then there was nothing. . . .

THIRTY-ONE

Ken Styles was having a hard time staying on his feet. His face felt as though it had been melted off his skull and drizzled back on like hot wax. Every step he took was more painful than the next and as much as he wanted to run away, he doubted his body was even capable of such activity.

He was used to being the one in charge. The one with all the answers. Even when Scotelli had started beating him, Styles figured his injuries were an acceptable inconvenience and all part of his plan. Now, stumbling down Main Street, he had to fight to keep his mind from screaming out of control.

New plans needed to be made to take the place of old ones. He knew that, but his skull felt like it had been cracked at some point during last night's trip into hell and thinking of even the simplest things was like walking a mile on two broken legs.

Somehow, he made it to the Three Aces. His walk into the saloon felt surreal, and his vision was starting to blur. It was through sheer will that he was able to stand up long enough to be noticed by one of the bouncers, who managed to catch him as he slumped sideways toward the bar.

"You all right?" one of the big men asked.

A familiar voice sounded from just out of his field of vision. "Is that you, Styles?"

The businessman looked up to see Greta's face before everything went black.

• • •

Even though there were a lot of boardinghouses on Bond Street, it wasn't hard for Clint to figure out which one to go to. True, it was one that seemed out of the way and situated on the corner, making it perfect for easy comings and goings. Also, it was a place with a good view of the street and all the people below it. But mainly, it was the screams and gunshots coming from one building in particular that really tipped him off.

When he heard the shots, he broke into a run. There were people running in every direction that led away from the house on the corner. As he got closer, Clint drew his gun, anticipating the worst. He was on the walk just outside the building when he heard footsteps from the narrow alley between the boardinghouse and a neighboring bakery.

The steps got louder and soon two men came around from behind the building. When the one in the lead saw Clint, he kept the gun in his hand pointed toward the ground. Cold, calm eyes studied Clint for a tense few seconds.

"Who are you?" Clint asked. His own pistol had been pointing at the men the instant they'd turned the corner, but it didn't seem to affect them.

Another set of footsteps came from inside the boardinghouse and soon, two more men stepped outside. Clint wouldn't allow himself to be flanked and so stepped away from the alley, putting his back to the bakery's wall. The two men emerging from the boardinghouse had the same cold detachment as the ones in the alley. They also looked Clint over, and then looked down the alley.

"We were just leaving," the lead man in the alley stated. He holstered his gun and then walked slowly into the street, being careful not to make any sudden moves. The rest followed suit, seeming to go out of their way not to provoke any hostility.

"What's going on in there?" Clint asked to any one of them.

"You'd better see for yourself."

Clint watched them leave, noting that they seemed to split off in four different directions. With his mind on full alert, he went into the boardinghouse and searched it. He hadn't come up with much more than a scared old woman until he went up the stairs and found one of the doors had been kicked off its hinges.

Inside that room was an empty chair sitting on top of a pile of cut ropes and the body of George Rainer slumped against the wall below the window. One bullet hole in his skull at the left temple. The expression on his face was one of quiet resignation; of a man who knew his death had come and had been powerless to stop it.

THIRTY-TWO

"I hope you'll excuse the mess," Greta said as Styles was helped into her office. "But one of your men shot this place up a bit last night, and I haven't had a chance to straighten up yet."

One of the Three Aces' bouncers dumped Styles into a chair, not seeming to mind the pained grunts coming from the businessman. After a nod from Greta, the bouncer turned and walked out the door, posting himself just outside in case he was needed in a rush.

Greta looked at Styles intently while he tried to find the position that hurt the least. "I got your message," she said. "So what is this about another payment?"

When Styles spoke, it sounded more like a croak. "I did plenty of good for you. Thanks to me and my men, you own three saloons across two states and have interests in at least a dozen more than that. You still owe me for the job in Wayne."

"I didn't hire you to burn places down in my name! You were supposed to be a business partner, but instead you turned out to be an extortionist and worse."

"That's part of the business," Styles spat. "You don't get your fingers on new prospects by holding your hands out and waiting for them to fall in. You go out and tear them away from those too weak to hold on to them, and if you're not strong enough to do that, you hire someone like me. This business gets dirtier the bigger it gets, just like any business, and don't you sit there and expect me to believe you knew nothing about it."

Greta sat behind her desk with her fingers steepled in front of her. "What happened to your face, Kenneth? Some of that dirty business come back to haunt you?"

Touching a finger to a swollen, discolored knob on his forehead, Styles winced in pain before leaning forward. "Actually, Mister Scotelli was a little more upset than I'd imagined. One plan backfires and you make another. If you had any business sense, you'd know that."

"Just skip to the point," she said in exasperation. "How much do you want so we can part ways and never do business again?"

Styles seemed to draw strength from the fact that the conversation had put him back into his own element. "I want your saloons. You can stay on as management, but I'll be the one in charge. I'll make all the decisions, and I'll get the majority of the profits."

Leaning back, Greta looked as though the words had smacked her across the face. "You can't be serious."

"I'm in too much pain to bullshit you, but the one thing that pulled me through was thinking about this moment. I want your saloons, and you're going to give them to me."

"This is what you had in mind all along, isn't it? Ever since the beginning, you've been waiting to make this move, haven't you?"

Styles shrugged. "That's what business is all about. You asked for my help so you could expand, and that's exactly what I'm doing. Expanding my interests. The main difference is that I think on a much larger scale than you do."

"What about what happened in Wayne? And killing Bobby Colville? Was all that part of you expanding your interests?"

"No. That was a way of protecting them. I worked for you the best way I knew how. But I could tell right from the start that you didn't have the stomach to go all the way in tearing through all the competition out there, especially in the saloon business. A town like Mandrake didn't have much to begin with, but when you start moving into other places, big or small, you've got to force your way in.

"I did that and succeeded. You didn't ask any questions when the money came in, which was the way it should have been."

"I didn't ask any questions because I didn't know about what you and your men were doing," Greta replied. "Funny how you seem to keep skipping over that part."

Styles waved his hand dismissively. The gesture seemed to cause him a fair amount of pain. "Be that as it may, what it boils down to is this. You sign over your saloons or your troubles start coming in by the dozens."

"Why not just take them from me like you did the others?"

"This is how I took the others, and I'll give you the same choice that everyone else was given. The only difference here is that I want this saloon intact. It would just be too expensive to rebuild. But make no mistake, if burning it down with you in it is what I need to do, I will do it."

Shaking her head, Greta felt as though her entire world had been turned upside down. "You're crazy. Do you know that?"

Styles started to laugh. Even though it hurt every one of his fractured ribs and made the pounding in his head more painful than when the pistol butts had been slammed against it, Styles couldn't help himself.

"If you knew just how much planning it took to get to this point, you'd appreciate how funny that statement was. I even shortchanged my associates in your name to get them riled up enough to come back here for you. The money I held back was put to good use in hiring better help. Except for a few—" he paused to rub a bloody ridge over his right eye "—bumps along the way, I'd say everything has gone pretty much as I wanted it. How crazy is that?"

"Did you plan on me calling on the sheriff and telling him about everything you just said, because that's exactly what I'm about to do."

"Actually, I did plan on that. In fact, I thought you'd get to it a lot sooner." Styles adjusted his position in the chair yet again. Whenever he got comfortable, he felt as if he was back in Scotelli's room with the ropes digging into his flesh. He needed the occasional movement to shake the creeping fear.

"I've been in your place enough times to make my presence known. Even this most recent time I came to town, your bartenders knew my drink and your serving girls didn't have to ask for my order. They know me. They know who I am, and they know I work for you." He leaned forward to tap a finger on Greta's desktop. "Those are your own workers. Think how many customers and associates there are who know the same thing. Hell, even Sheriff Cole knows my association with you. If you turn me in, you're only drawing the law down onto you as well. It's your word against mine whether I was or was not taking orders from you to have those people killed or have those buildings put to the torch. Are you ready to prove to a court of law that you didn't give me those orders?"

Now Greta leaned forward and smacked the businessman's hand off of her desk. "If you want to force my hand, you can sure as hell try. I talk with plenty of types every night, and I can pay some of them just as easily to get rid of you for a whole lot less than giving away my livelihood."

"Ahhh, now you're getting a head for business. I knew that you would come to your senses eventually."

"You're right. I have come to my senses. You remember that man you saw with me earlier? The one who chased your two out of here like a couple of scalded dogs? He's been looking for you, and now I can give you to him. You want to send those two back in here? Well, if Clint isn't here, I've got plenty of my own men working for me that know they'll be coming and will be waiting for you."

Greta felt the rage churning inside of her. It brought her to her feet and nearly caused her to reach over and throttle Styles with her bare hands. "Billy!" she yelled.

In response to her call, the hulking bouncer outside opened the door and stepped in. "Yes, Miss Ulrich?"

"Take this gentleman and put him in a room upstairs. Don't let him leave. Give him a few more bruises if you must."

Even though Billy had known Styles for the better part of a year, he seemed more than pleased at the thought of sinking his fists into the well-dressed man. Without a word, he grabbed hold of Styles and brought him to his feet.

"It's not Scotelli and Rainer you have to worry about,"

Styles said through a pain great enough to twist his stomach into knots.

Motioning for Billy to wait, Greta stepped around her desk to look into the businessman's face. "What do you mean?"

"They're gone. If they're still in town at all, they're dead in the street thanks to the men I purchased with your money to help me with this takeover. Men who won't make mistakes like what happened in Wayne. They were good enough to find me and rescue me from Scotelli. They'll find me again!"

"Take him away, Billy," Greta said, her face etched with the disgust she felt for Styles.

"Do what you want now," Styles said as he was being dragged away. "By this time tomorrow, when you look at me, you'll be looking at the sole proprietor of both the Three Aces and Prairie Dog saloons. I'll be a rich man! Rich enough to buy a fancy funeral for you or anyone else who doesn't step quickly out of my way!"

THIRTY-THREE

Clint burst into the Three Aces and could hear Styles ranting over the growing commotion of the lunch crowd. Making his way toward the back, he watched as two bouncers as big around as oak trees pulled Styles up the stairs with the businessman's heels dragging on the ground. He then turned to the office and found Greta already waiting in the doorway.

"I think he's still going to be a problem," she said, indicating Styles.

Clint grabbed her by the wrist and pulled her into the office. "More than you know." As quick as he could, he filled her in on what he'd been doing. When he told her about the body he'd found in the boardinghouse and the four men that had been there, Greta made her way to the closest chair, which was the same one that had just been vacated by Styles.

"Those four men were hired by Styles," she said.

"How do you know?"

Greta filled him in on the high points of her conversation with Styles, including his threat at the end. "He told me that anyone who got in his way would be dead. Including me and Maddy."

"But why would he hire men to kill the men he had already bought?"

Greta walked behind her desk and removed a slip of paper

from one of the drawers. "Here," she said while handing it over. "Maybe this could explain it."

Before he even got a chance to look at it, Clint had a pretty good idea what the paper was. Sure enough, it was a message addressed to Greta as well as Madeline Lowell.

STYLES IS WITH US
HE DIES UNLESS WE GET OUR MONEY
THEN YOU ARE NEXT
SCOTELLI

"So they kidnapped their own boss to get their money?" Clint shook his head. "That doesn't make a lot of sense."

"They didn't kidnap anybody. Styles was afraid of getting caught now that everything he's done is out in the open. He ran to those two for protection and thought they'd be enough to keep him safe until his real help got here."

"Real help? You mean those four I saw at the boarding-house?"

Greta shrugged. "I don't really know. The first I heard about any other hired guns was just a few minutes ago. I halfway thought Styles was bluffing. Trying to scare me."

"If he was talking about those men I saw, he definitely wasn't bluffing. I've seen a lot of gunmen in my time, those four had the look of professionals. That room was pretty shot up, but the man they killed only had one hole in him. That means whoever killed him was quick, precise, and calm under fire. That's the mark of a pro."

Easing herself into her chair, Greta looked toward the ceiling and then nervously down at her hands. "Clint, what are we going to do? All I wanted was a successful business, and I wind up getting mixed up in shootings and burning people out of their homes. Then I meet you and almost get you killed also."

Clint walked around to sit on the edge of her desk. He reached down to hold both her hands and looked into her eyes. "The whole problem so far has been that none of us really knew what we were dealing with. Now we know that Styles is crazy enough to kill for the sake of swinging a deal the right way, and he's going to keep killing as long as he sees a profit in it."

"But what about the men he's hired? They won't stop until I hand over my life's work or I'm dead."

"Those men may be the guns, but Styles is the one pulling the trigger. Professional killers are the most dangerous kind of scum, but they wouldn't have done any of this if it hadn't been for the man paying them. I'll deal with those four, but the most important thing is for you to make sure you keep hold of Styles. Now, can you trust those men you have watching him?"

"The biggest one's my brother. The rest know better than to cross him, so yeah, I can trust them. Maybe we should just give him to the sheriff."

"No," Clint said. "I'd feel better with him right here. He wouldn't try to do anything to the saloon while he was in it. Besides, I doubt your sheriff could do much to those four other than ask them to please hand over their guns."

Greta's laugh was uncomfortable, but genuine. When she reached out to hold Clint, her entire body was shaking. She gently placed her head on his lap and closed her eyes. "Thank you for everything you've done to help me. And for believing me."

He ran his hand over the smooth gold of her hair and put a finger beneath her chin so he could bring her eyes up to meet his. "I've still got my suspicions about all of this, but don't take it personally. I've been in the way of more bullets in the last few days than I care to think about and every time I think I've got this all figured out, some other twist comes down the path. I want you to do me a favor and give me a few minutes alone with Styles. I think if I can talk to him, I can clear a lot of things up."

"I told you everything he said. Don't you trust me?"

"That's got nothing to do with it," he said, even though that wasn't the complete truth. "I need to look into his eyes and hear him say it in his own words. You can tell more about a man by paying attention to what's going on in his eyes than what's coming out of his mouth."

More than anything, Clint wanted to take Greta's story at face value. But he hadn't lived so long in his kind of life by trusting every soul that asked him to. Beside, he wasn't lying about wanting to look into Styles's eyes one more time. He'd played poker with the man and knew his tells. Clint would know the cards Styles was holding whether or not the businessman showed him his hand.

"I won't be long," he said, while bending down to give her a quick kiss on the lips.

When he tried to pull away, she reached up and held the back of his head. Her lips pressed against his with a passion that kept him in his spot. He could feel her mouth opening, and he allowed her tongue to mingle with his own. They pulled away at the same time, and her hand drifted along his cheek.

"Be careful," she said. "Just promise me that."

"I'm only going upstairs, Greta. Not off to war."

"I just can't stop thinking about how quickly things have happened lately. As soon as I think I'm safe and in control, someone kicks down my door and starts shooting. You even got ambushed when you were checking on your horse. I don't feel safe anymore. Not unless you're near me."

"I promise I'll be right back. What I want to know, I'll be able to find out quickly."

THIRTY-FOUR

Clint went up the stairs and headed for the door with the two buffaloes in black vests standing in front of it. Having seen him being taken into Miss Ulrich's confidence more than once, the bouncers took a step to the side and let him pass. Clint opened the door to find a room not unlike his own, but with the bed shoved to one side and the writing desk pushed into a corner.

Styles sat tied to a chair in the space that had been cleared in the middle of the room. The businessman looked as though he'd been dropped out of a few second-floor windows, and one of his eyes was nearly swollen shut. His expensive suit was stained with dried blood and damp with sweat.

"Does that feel familiar?" Clint asked. The picture of what he'd found in the boardinghouse room filled his mind.

His head hung low, Styles barely managed to look up when he answered. "Sure, and I guess you know what happened to the last ones that tried this."

"You mean Scotelli?"

"That's right. They should be finding him any minute. Then they'll come after you."

"I guess by *they,* you mean those four gun hands I passed on my way over here?"

Styles nodded. His eyes were wide from pain and something else that brought quick breaths to him in short bursts. Just as quickly as his fits came, they were gone. Clint had seen people act like this before, and they'd all been tied up for good reason.

"You thought you had Scotelli all figured out, didn't you?" Clint asked as he stepped closer to watch the other man's face.

"He was stupid."

"But you knew he was going to burn down that saloon in Wayne along with most of the town, didn't you?"

Styles paused and thought for a second. "No . . . I didn't . . ." He started to drift off as though his brain was elsewhere.

Clint was still watching closely, not really listening to the words, but watching Styles's face as intently as he would at a high-stakes game. The businessman was giving himself away with every facial tick and each nervous fidget.

"Those ropes I saw at the boardinghouse," Clint said slowly. "They were cut. Those men had to rescue you, and then you came running back here, but Scotelli got away, didn't he?"

Another nervous shift of the feet.

Clint watched the man's body language and pressed on. "I'll bet you came here for the same reason you went to Scotelli . . . for protection. Except now you need protecting from him until he's found. How long before those four come to bust you out of here?" Now Clint positioned himself so that he was staring straight into Styles's eyes and drew his gun. "Do you really think they'll care if they find a dead body?"

The panic set in all over again.

"I can pay you," Styles whined. "I can't stop what's going to happen, but if you let me go I might be able to save Greta's life. I can save both of them. It's only business. It's only business!"

"You can keep your business. I just got all from you that I needed."

With that, Clint turned and walked out of the room, ignoring the rants and raves coming from the man behind him. When he got outside, the bouncers seemed to look to him for their next set of orders.

"Are you armed?" Clint asked.

With a confident smirk, the two gorillas peeled back their vests to show the guns they had strapped beneath them.

"Well, get some shotguns," Clint said as he headed for the

stairs. "And if you see anyone dangerous coming toward you, don't hesitate to use them."

He took the stairs two at a time and swung around the corner into Greta's office. One of the bartenders was in there with her. Greta seemed to be back to her normal self and was issuing strict commands to her worker. Clint took hold of her arm and eased her away.

"We're leaving," he said tersely.

"What? Where are we going?"

"You'll find out when you get there, just come with me right now."

With Greta in tow, Clint went straight through the saloon's crowd and out the door. On the way, she was shouting out to the workers she passed, telling them quickly that she would be gone for a while and to keep on the lookout. Some of the customers got nervous when they heard her and a few of them even started making their own way to the door.

"This had better be important," she warned when she saw the scared patrons. "This is costing me money."

When they were on the street, Clint kept walking until he was able to pull her close and talk without having anyone close enough to overhear. "Well, if you stayed there much longer, it might have cost you your life."

"What? But I've got plenty of guards and Styles wouldn't be crazy enough to—"

"I talked to him and read his face. Believe me, he's got enough confidence mixed in with his craziness to be a dangerous man. He even slipped and told me he'd signed your death warrants."

"Oh, my God. I guess I never really thought he'd have the nerve to back up his threats."

"He's got plenty of nerve. Plus he's got new shooters in town to back his play."

They'd been heading north, away from Main Street. Clint was just trying to get Greta away from the Three Aces, but now he needed a more specific destination.

"Where's another hotel in town besides the Prairie Dog?"

"There's the Mandrake Inn, but I'm not sure if it's even open anymore."

"Does Styles know about it?"

Greta shook her head. "I told him the saloons were successful enough to close down their competition when we first met. I was trying to impress him into agreeing to work with me."

"No problem there," Clint said sarcastically. "Where is it?"

She told him how to get there. It was only two streets over in one of the older parts of town.

Clint saw her to the corner and gave her a quick hug. "Go in there and get a room. Will the hotel owner recognize you?"

"Probably, but we're not on bad terms."

"Will he tell anyone you're there?"

"He may not like my saloon taking away his customers, but he doesn't want me dead. Where are you going?"

"Over to the Prairie Dog. I've got to get to the next woman on Styles's list."

THIRTY-FIVE

Although he'd only been in town a few days, Clint already knew the floor plan and peak hours of both of the big saloons in Mandrake. He knew the Prairie Dog wouldn't be as busy as the Three Aces at this time of the afternoon since most of the Dog's patrons were more of the nighttime drinking variety. Walking into the saloon on Third Street, Clint saw immediately that he'd figured right.

Tossing a wave to the bartenders, Clint made his way quickly to the hotel desk in the back and was glad to find Maddy waiting at the counter. The smile on her face grew wider the closer he got.

"Great to see you," she said warmly. "I knew you'd make the right decision once you had a chance to compare."

Clint walked around the desk and up the stairs to her office. Waving her inside, he looked down at the saloon to scan for any trace of the four men he'd seen on Bond Street. With the crowd as thin as it was, there wasn't a lot of places to hide, and Clint was fairly certain he'd beaten them there.

"Anything happen while I was gone?" Clint asked after closing the door.

Maddy tossed her hair over her shoulders and bent over her desk. "Not a lot besides this." She grabbed a slip of paper from her top drawer and handed it over.

Clint looked at it just long enough to make sure it was what he thought it was. "Greta got one of these, too," he said, giving back the letter. "Anything else you want to tell me?"

"Weeeelll . . ." Maddy sounded like a guilty child, and she cringed while stepping around the desk so it was between her and Clint.

"Come on, spill it."

"I kind of already knew that Styles was going to that boardinghouse. I was the one who paid Scotelli and Rainer to keep hold of him and rough him up a little."

By no means had Clint seen that one coming. Still, he tried to keep the utter shock from registering on his face.

"Why would you do that? I thought Scotelli was working for Greta."

"He was. They all were, but a few weeks ago, that Styles character approached me and asked if I was willing to sell my Prairie Dog. I told him to get stuffed, and he sent in Scotelli to put the scare into me."

"Sounds about right."

"Well, I don't scare like most folks, so I did the best thing I could think of. I doubled the money she was paying them and told them to keep their mouths shut. I've been paying them ever since as sort of an ace up my sleeve until the time was right. Rainer came to me when they got to town the other night and told me Scotelli was gunning for Styles and Greta. We may have some heavy competition between us, but I don't hate her enough to see her dead. Not to mention that I couldn't believe Greta would work with a slimy rodent like Styles."

Suddenly, Clint had a better idea at who was more cut out for the rougher side of the saloon business.

"Anyway," she continued, "when I heard from Rainer, I told him that if they hadn't gotten their money, it was Styles's fault and not Greta's. She's one of the few people I know that don't have any debts."

"What else did you tell him?"

At first, Maddy shrugged as if she hadn't a clue as to what Clint could possibly mean. But after he stared her down, she held her hands out to the sides.

"All right! I might have told him I'd throw in a bonus if they made Styles sorry that he'd ever set foot in Mandrake."

Clint couldn't help but laugh at the notion that the big, tough businessman, who owned gunhands the way others owned hats, had got his tail kicked in at the order of a woman. A woman, by the way, whom Styles was getting ready to run out of her own town. Sometimes deals aren't as easy as they should be. Clint was familiar with that kind of business.

"I'm sure you'd be pleased if you got a look at Styles's face," Clint said.

Maddy got a mischievous twinkle in her eye and stepped a little closer to him. "Yeah?" She reached out and traced her fingers down his chest. "So you're not mad about what I did?"

"No, but I need to get you out of here. I already put Greta in a room down at the Mandrake Inn—"

"Is that place still in business?"

"It's not the fanciest place, but it's somewhere Styles doesn't know about, which means his men probably don't know about it either. I'll take you there, but we've got to leave now before they come looking."

Maddy led the way from the office and into her room. "You're sure they're coming for me?" she asked while throwing a few pieces of clothing into a carpetbag.

"You tell me. He wants both your saloon and Greta's, and he's already threatened you both. Now, he brings in the second set of killers to take care of the job. That sounds pretty bad to me."

Clint watched as Maddy finished packing. She was standing near her dresser by the window, so he took her by the elbow and led her away from the glass. "Don't give them a clean shot. I shouldn't have even wasted time doing this," he said.

"I wasn't about to go anywhere without my things."

"Are you ready now?"

"Not quite." She threw herself into his arms and kissed him long and passionately on the mouth. Her tongue licked his lips and then flicked between them. Her fingers ran through Clint's hair, sending a chill down his spine. When she pulled away, she reveled in the distraction she'd caused.

"Now I'm ready."

After Clint saw Maddy safely to the hotel, he took a roundabout way back to the center of town so that his arrival wouldn't give away the direction he'd come from. He knew three things for sure: First, Scotelli was supposed to be dead in that boardinghouse, but had gotten away. Second, the four shooters had fanned out to look for him. And third, he needed to put all of those men out of the picture one way or another to end this business for good.

Clint checked to make sure he had plenty of spare ammunition and that his gun was fully loaded.

It was time to hunt the hunters.

THIRTY-SIX

Pete Scotelli had made enough circles around town to learn every alley and backstreet better than if he'd lived there his entire life. As much as he wanted to sit and rest for a while, he could always hear the steady, heavy footsteps of those steely-eyed men who remained constantly on his heels.

He'd first seen them when he was returning to the boardinghouse on his way back from the Prairie Dog Saloon. He watched them go in and figured he would wait and attack them when they were driven out. But when they came out, it was too late. Scotelli didn't hear much of anything besides Rainer's frantic shots and the final crack of a pistol that ended his partner's cries.

When they'd filed out of the boardinghouse, they spotted him instantly and the sight of them had sparked something primitive in Scotelli's soul. Something deep inside told him to run. He'd never heard that voice before and his hesitance had nearly cost him his life.

The first one drew and fired quicker than Scotelli could blink. The only thing that saved him was the way he'd been standing and the narrowness of his frame. Scotelli had positioned himself so that his shoulders lined up facing the house's door, making himself a smaller target. The bullet tore through the front of his jacket and dug a shallow trench across his chest, which caused more pain than real damage. Spurred by the near miss, Scotelli ran for cover and lost himself in the frightened crowd.

Again, thanks to his narrow build, he'd been able to shove himself through a broken fence and into a loose back door that only he and nobody above the age of twelve would have been able to get through. His shortcuts had ripped up his clothes and aggravated his deep scratch, but they'd also put enough distance between himself and the four killers to give them the slip.

At least for now.

He'd been running ever since then, but the time on his feet had allowed him to come up with a plan. Every time he circled past one of the large saloons, Scotelli thought about going in. He almost made it inside the Prairie Dog before he thought he'd heard the sound of approaching footsteps.

The one he really wanted to get into was the Three Aces. That was where he knew he could find at least one of the two people he wanted to see dead. Ulrich was always in there, and Styles would most likely be there, too. He owed them both for cheating him out of his money as well as his life, and he didn't much care which one he got his hands on first.

It would be dark out soon, which meant hiding would be easier and so would moving around. He always liked working in the dark. Killing just felt better when the sun was down.

A board squeaked on the walk just outside the alley Scotelli was hiding in, which made his stomach clench into a tight ball. As he scurried deeper into the shadows, he thought he heard movement coming from there as well.

Maybe the dark wasn't so great after all.

The man at the table went by Nolan. If you knew him by name, you were either paying for his services or one of his men. Other than that, he was just another man sitting alone at a table in a saloon.

He sat in the back of the Three Aces Saloon, nursing the same drink he'd ordered two hours ago. The place was coming to life around him. Showgirls were beginning to prance across the raised platform stage, more of the gambling tables were being used, and less of the bar could be seen through the row of drinkers leaning against the polished wood.

The serving girl had stopped coming up to ask him about his next drink when he'd finally fixed her with an intense glare. She'd apologized, turned quickly away, and he hadn't seen her since. All the better. When he was on a job, he didn't drink heavily. None of his men did.

That's what people expected when they hired him and his crew. They were the best.

He hadn't seen much since Styles had been dragged upstairs, kicking and screaming like a crazy woman. Adams had followed him up shortly after that and then came down alone. The man at the table knew enough about Clint Adams to know he hadn't done much to Styles when he was up there. The Gunsmith was a famous man, but not for being an executioner.

No, the man thought as he took a small sip off the top of his whiskey, Styles was still alive and well. Maybe a little worse for wear, but alive.

The man at the table was dressed simply. Black pants, white shirt with no tie, and a black riding coat that hung down to his knees. The coat was big enough to cover the pistol and double-barreled shotgun that were strapped beneath his shoulders, yet short enough to stay out of his way when the guns were needed. And they would be needed on this job, just like every other.

His eyes were what most people remembered about him. Nolan and all his men had had the compassion burned out of them years ago in their dealings with war, tragedy, and so many encounters with death that they were all dead themselves. He wouldn't have it any other way. That's what gave them the intensity in their eyes and the purpose in their walk. Between himself and his crew, the five men had seen every form of cruelty known to man. They'd even made up a few of their own when the job had required it.

This job wouldn't require anything so special. It was a simple mop-up detail that required one person to be standing when it was over. That person was now being held upstairs in one of the saloon's hotel rooms, so before long the man at the table would go up there and break him out. His men had done it before, earlier in the day, so what was once more?

Looking at his watch, he pondered if he should just go up

there, slaughter those guards, and get the hell away from the deafening noise of the drinking crowd.

No, he decided. Give the men a little while longer to find Scotelli. Nolan still had a drink to finish.

THIRTY-SEVEN

Mandrake seemed to become a whole lot bigger to Clint once he began walking its side streets and alleyways looking for a single man who didn't want to be found. He wasn't about to wander aimlessly until he heard gunshots because then it would be too late. The only way he could be certain of drawing out all four of those men was to make sure Scotelli stayed alive to act as bait. As long as that happened, every one of those men would come after him, which distracted them from the task of killing Greta and Maddy.

First, however, he had to find Scotelli. He couldn't do that thinking as he normally would. Clint needed to start thinking like a fugitive. Had to get the blood flowing quick in his veins and feel the fearful chill of being hunted. Had to get the right mixture of panic and cunning in his own mind in order to get a clue as to what was going on in Scotelli's.

The first thing that a hunted man would want to do would be to keep moving until he'd found a safe enough place to hole up. Clint thought about the door in the boardinghouse that had been knocked clean off its hinges, and the single hole in Rainer's forehead. Scotelli wouldn't be going anywhere near that part of town.

Who had brought him and Rainer to Mandrake in the first place?

Who had brought the four shooters into this business?

Who was the next best bait that Clint already knew where to find?

Styles.

At least the well-dressed weasel was good for something.

Clint stuck to the shadows as he headed back toward the Three Aces, keeping his eyes and ears open for the first sign of movement coming from any direction. His gun filled his hand without him even thinking about drawing it, and his posture had become crooked and stooped while trying to scurry from alley to alley, ducking behind buildings and keeping his head down, trying to make himself look smaller.

Perhaps one of the four gunmen might just mistake him for Scotelli. Clint was only halfway to Main Street before his charade paid off.

He'd been keeping away from the wooden walkways on either side of the bigger streets so he wouldn't be putting any townspeople in danger. Clint was behind a darkened clothing store when he heard a boot slowly crunching against a patch of loose gravel behind him. Spinning around, Clint stepped sideways and plastered his back against the rear wall of the store as a gun went off from the direction of the footstep.

Clint heard the bullet rip through the space he'd just cleared and switched his pistol to his left hand so he could take aim without moving away from the wall. He wasn't as good firing with his other hand, but he was good enough to thumb the hammer, raise his arm, and fire while only losing a fraction of a second off his speed.

Clint's shot went wide, but not by much. With his ears straining for every noise they could get ahold of, he could hear the sound of lead slapping against wood and a whispered curse coming from the next lot.

Not wasting a second of the few he'd just bought, Clint ducked behind a small set of steps that led up to the back door of the store. Another wild shot rang out from the next lot over and then another. It was at that moment that Clint knew he was not dealing with one of the professionals.

"Come on out, Scotelli," he called. "I'm not here to kill you."

"Then why did you just shoot at me?"

"Just returning the favor. Now come over here before I do start coming for you."

Peering around the steps, Clint watched as Scotelli stepped tentatively from the shadows. The Italian held his gun stiff-armed in front of him. A thin smile was plastered across his lips.

When the other man was fully in sight, Clint stood without shifting his aim. He noticed Scotelli looking him over as he walked forward.

"How'd you find me?"

Clint shrugged. "It wasn't hard. The way I see it, you don't have a lot of places to go. You're not the type to leave town even if it's the best thing for you."

"Damn right I'm not leavin'. Not after what happened to George. Styles is gonna pay in blood, not to mention the rest of what he owes me."

"I'd say you've got bigger problems than Styles right now. Four of them to be exact."

"One's all it's gonna take."

Those last words came from the alley between both buildings, causing Clint and Scotelli to swivel at the same time to face who'd spoken them.

Before he saw the man, Clint knew who it would be. The third man stood in the middle of the alley as if he were just out for a nightly stroll. Dressed in simple clothes and a brown coat, he stood with his shoulders relaxed and his arms hanging loose at his sides. If it weren't for the cold, dead eyes that were wedged into his face like they'd been shot from a musket, he might have been mistaken for nothing more than a bystander.

Scotelli forgot about Clint and everything that had taken place before this moment. He squared off against the man in the alley, not sure whether it would be stupid to let his arm drop or if he was quick enough to raise it the rest of the way for him to take his shot. Instead, he stood there with his pistol aimed at the ground between them, the look of a cornered animal on his sunken features.

Clint watched for any sign of movement in the third man and found nothing besides the motion of the breeze kicking at the edges of his coat. It was his stillness that told Clint the most. It told him that he needed to make his own move damn quick.

"Where are the others?" Clint asked.

The man didn't take his eyes off of Scotelli. Watching him talk was like seeing the lips on a statue move. "They're coming."

"I figured, since it took four of you to shoot one man back at the boardinghouse."

The dig had no effect. Not even a twitch.

Clint took a step out away from the steps, giving him some space to move. As soon as he did, the man snapped his coat open with one hand to show the double rig strapped high around the waist. Only show-offs wore their guns low. The real shootists kept them high so they could draw and pull back the hammer in one move.

Waiting for the last possible second, Clint twisted sideways while keeping his arm close to his midsection. The swift motion looked effortless, but was more than enough for him to aim and get a shot off. The man in the alley was fast. Fast enough to get his hands to his guns and clear leather, but not before Clint's bullet slammed through the middle of his heart and knocked him off his feet.

Both of the man's guns went off in his clenched fists, kicking up two mounds in the dirt. Keeping his body turned, Clint walked over to the man to make sure he'd finished the job.

"Jesus almighty, that was fast!" Scotelli blurted out.

Clint looked over to check Scotelli's position and found the other man pointing his gun at the fallen man. Walking over to the body, Clint kept his distance since both guns were still firmly in his grasp. Those cold eyes were wide open and staring at the sky, looking no more dead now than they had when he'd been up and walking.

As Clint got closer, he heard the man's last breath slip from his mouth. Only then did his muscles relax enough for him to give up his weapons.

Scotelli was standing next to him when Clint bent down to pick up the guns and toss them out of sight.

"One down, three to go," the Italian said. "Then . . . Styles dies."

Clint turned on him only slightly slower than he had seconds ago when firing. "Back off!"

Scotelli didn't look surprised. The smug expression on his face only grew more sickening the farther away he got. "Did that bitch pay you to kill me, or did she just fuck you until you agreed to hunt me down?"

"Throw your gun on the ground and kick it to me."

Scotelli did as he was told and raised his hands in the air. All the fight that had been in him had disappeared after seeing Clint out-shoot one of the killers he'd been running from all night. But it was pride that kept him from going quietly. "I've seen some cheap bastards in my time, but Styles takes the cake. I ain't never even heard of someone going through so much trouble to get away with shortchanging a man for an easy job."

"Move that out of the alley," Clint said while pointing to the body. Now he had both his and Scotelli's gun in either hand. "Get it out of sight."

Disgusted more by the manual labor than by the sight of the fresh corpse, Scotelli reached down and grabbed hold of both dead legs and started dragging the man behind the stairs that Clint had been using for cover. "So what now?" he asked when he was done.

Clint stepped back until he was covered in shadow and tossed over the Italian's gun. "Now you're going to start running."

THIRTY-EIGHT

Scotelli was getting tired. Even from his vantage point fifty feet behind him, Clint could tell that. At first, he wasn't sure the Italian would do as he was told, but he seemed more than happy to put some distance between himself, Clint, and the body he'd shoved under a staircase.

He was heading for the Three Aces, just as he had been before. Clint was keeping pace with him, making sure to keep a good distance behind him while watching for any of the three remaining shooters. He knew they'd be making their way toward the sound of gunfire and just when Clint was starting to wonder what was taking them so long, another of the dead-eyed killers stepped into view.

Scotelli stopped as though his feet had instantly grown roots. He was at the end of Fifth Street where it intersected with Main. The man he was looking at stood on the walkway made of warped planks in front of a row of dark storefronts. Clint moved into an alley three buildings away. There were still some pedestrians about, heading for the saloon, and when they saw the two men with guns they quickly began to scatter.

Clint used the movement of people for cover as he worked his way to another alley across the street and one building away from the nameless gunman.

This one, unlike the one he'd faced down earlier, wasn't in the mood to talk, no matter how much Scotelli was trying to bait him. The quiet one looked similar in build to the others, but was dressed in more rugged clothing. He looked like he'd just gotten off the trail in his dusty pants, denim shirt, and at least a month's worth of beard covering his face. He only had one gun, which was also strapped high around the hips.

As Clint got closer, he could hear Scotelli taunting the other man, but didn't care to listen to what was being said. Rather than join into the one-sided conversation, Clint moved up as close as he could get without being seen and then stepped into the street. He could feel more than see the gunman's eyes flick in his direction.

"One of your partners is dead," Clint said as he squared off against the bearded man. "You'll join him unless you turn around and leave town now."

Beneath the beard, the other man's jaw started to move as though he was slowly gnawing on something. "You work for him?" he asked with a nod of his head, motioning toward Scotelli.

"I don't work for anyone," Clint replied. "But you're coming in on a bigger mess than you know."

"That's what we get paid for."

Clint eased his hand down toward the gun at his side. "Whatever it is Styles is giving you, it isn't enough."

And at that moment, Clint knew he'd spent too much time talking.

As soon as he heard the slow, steady footsteps moving in behind him, Clint spun around in a half-circle while drawing his gun at the same time. In the next second, three shots blasted through the night. The first came from another one of the silent killers that had walked up from the same alley Clint had used less than a minute ago. The second came from the man aiming at Scotelli, and the third was fired by Clint himself.

With his mind trying to get him out of the way of at least one incoming bullet, Clint let his instincts take control of his body and continued in his spin until he was again facing the shooter on the corner. The bullet from the alley took a bite from his shoulder, but it wasn't even as bad as the scratch on his neck.

Another gunshot sounded, and Scotelli dropped to the ground. He was still moving, but painfully so.

Clint squeezed off a shot into the first gunman and took a step into the street while looking over his shoulder to check the alley. At first, he didn't see any sign of the second killer. Then he caught a glimpse of motion on the other side of the street, and when he turned to face it, the man he'd been looking for straightened up and raised his gun.

Clint sacrificed his aim for his life as he fired off a few rounds to cover himself as he ducked into the alley. He could hear Scotelli grunting in pain as well as the steady, pounding steps of the bearded man as he climbed down off the sidewalk and into the street.

Glimpsing around the corner, Clint saw Scotelli crawling toward the opposite side of the street, still trying to fire the pistol that had been emptied a few minutes ago before Clint handed it back. The bearded man was walking after him, his left side dark and glistening with fresh blood. Directly across from Clint was the other gunman, who stared back at him hard enough for Clint to feel the man's gaze as if they were icicles stabbing him.

Turning to face the one across from him, Clint felt a twinge of pain in his ribs. It was the hot stabbing kind of pain brought by a gunshot wound, and knowing that, he pushed it to the back of his mind so he could keep from getting another in a more vital area.

Even though the gunman was across the street, Clint had no trouble focusing in on the shooter's eyes. He concentrated on them and nothing else.

All sound was blocked from his mind. The burning pain in his ribs was forgotten and nothing was left in Mandrake but those cold, dead eyes.

They didn't move.

They didn't blink.

They narrowed slightly . . . and Clint fired.

At the first sign of motion, the killer snapped his hand up, aimed, and pulled the trigger. But Clint was one step ahead of him and by the time the other man's hammer had fallen against the brass casing, Clint's lead had already made a tunnel through the killer's skull. The death reflex caused his finger to clench around the trigger even harder, which pulled the pistol high and to the right, sending a bullet to the stars.

Clint stepped back out into the street to find the bearded man had been watching the scene play itself out. His gun was trained on Scotelli, who was still on the ground.

"Let him go," Clint warned.

"What's he mean to you?" the bearded man asked. "You're not the law."

"He's got to serve as an example. These killings have to stop, and he needs to be given to the law so he can tell everything he knows to a judge. That way everyone gets what's coming to them . . . including Styles."

"I let him go, that makes me look bad. We don't back out on contracts."

"Let me guess," Clint said with exasperation tainting his voice. "It's business, right?"

"That's right."

"Well, the man who hired you isn't in any position to pay. Just ask him," Clint said while pointing to Scotelli.

The bearded man was motionless. His eyes held solidly on Clint, his gun on Scotelli.

The Italian was squirming on the ground. He'd been shot, but it was hard to tell how bad it was. Scotelli crawled another few feet and then let himself fall on his face, letting out a pained grunt when he hit the ground.

Clint and the bearded man stared at each other for what felt like forever. Each man waited for the other to make his move.

Inside, the quiet killer chose a maneuver that had gotten him out of similar predicaments in the past. He started to move into a well-practiced dodge, already focusing in on how he would kill the man who'd killed his partners.

Having found the single weakness in the silent gunmen, Clint zeroed in on the eyes of the bearded man, and as soon as they made the slightest change, he fired. Even with his early warning, Clint was barely able to stop the killer before he'd brought his gun around to bear on him. When the hired gun dropped, a fresh hole smoking in his chest, his hand had come around and was beginning to pull the trigger. A second later, the pistol landed heavily on the ground.

Anyone but The Gunsmith would have been dead where they stood.

THIRTY-NINE

Clint took his time getting to the Three Aces, hoping the last of the four men he'd seen would show themselves and be done with it. Scotelli was hurt, but the wound would heal once it was treated. Besides, Clint figured a little pain was good penance for a man responsible for as much as Scotelli was.

When he got to the saloon, Clint found the doctor at his usual table and dumped Scotelli in a seat next to him.

"He's been shot," Clint said, too tired to say much of anything else.

The doctor looked appalled at the way the wounded man was treated, but knew better than to discuss it with Clint. Instead, he shot a disgusted look toward him and rounded up a few warm bodies from the poker players to help him get Scotelli to an upstairs room. By the time the doctor and his patient were gone, most everyone in the place had returned to their own business.

Clint walked over to the bar and flagged down one of the men in vests behind it. "Send for the sheriff," he said to the bartender.

The rotund man didn't even put down the glass he was polishing. "Already sent someone for him. I recognized that one when you brought him in. Heard the shooting, too. What'll I tell Sheriff Cole when he wants to talk to you?"

"Tell him I'll find him tomorrow. Has anyone been asking for Miss Ulrich?"

"Nope. Besides, having her gone and a prisoner upstairs, it seems like business as usual around here. Mind if I ask where Miss Ulrich is?"

"You can ask, but I don't think it's a good idea for me to tell you. Just know that she's fine and safer where she's at than here." Clint turned and scanned the room. He was actually getting used to the commotion that was normal for the saloon and many of the faces were starting to look familiar.

Turning back to the bartender, Clint asked, "Is Styles giving anyone any trouble?"

"I think he's enjoying all the attention, but he seems pretty quiet."

"Hard to say if that's good or bad. I'll be right back."

As soon as Clint walked away, the bartender was flagged down by a thirsty customer. Clint headed back toward the staircase and climbed up to the hotel rooms, taking note of how many people were hanging around that area and how tight the security was. When he got to the top, he found everything was as he'd left it. One bouncer at the head of the stairs and two of the biggest ones standing by the door.

He asked a few questions and took a peek inside Styles's room, finding nothing worth getting upset about. In fact, the better it looked here, the more Clint wanted to get back to the ladies and make sure that the remaining gunman wasn't getting a free shot while he was gone.

"Where's the back door to this place?" Clint asked one of the bouncers.

The mountainous youth jabbed a finger toward the end of the hall, where two suites sat across from each other. Next to the door on the left was a narrower entrance that would even be a tight squeeze for Greta to get through. "Little door leads to some stairs," the bouncer said. "Watch your head."

It opened onto a cramped stairway that had less room to maneuver than a closet. He had to angle his body the entire time to keep from knocking himself silly against the walls on the way down, and at the bottom was another door that was held shut by a well-oiled latch, which opened silently on smooth hinges. He found himself behind the saloon facing the back end of a row of what appeared to be some of the neighboring gambling halls.

Clint hoped that if anyone had been watching him go up the stairs, they would think he was still up there. The ruse wouldn't last for long, if it was even needed. As he headed toward the Mandrake Inn, Clint felt the events of the last few days weighing on him even more. It was all certainly more than he'd bargained for, but then again, he should have known he'd be running into a lot more than a few firebugs.

What it all boiled down to was Styles, Maddy, and Greta. Styles was the one hiring all the guns, and with most of those guns dead, the businessman would be out of business once all his dealings came to the attention of the law. At least others would know what they were dealing with when they heard the name Kenneth Styles. At best, Styles would rot away in a little cell somewhere long enough for his money to dry up. That, for a businessman, was worse than death.

Maddy and Greta were not killers. Clint knew that by talking with them and seeing how they'd reacted to this whole mess. The simple fact that Styles wanted them dead as much as he wanted their saloons proved that they were not in league with him. Hopefully, after all this was over, they would be happier with the fortune they'd already made for themselves. All Clint had to do now was keep them alive long enough for him to clear out the murderous element of Mandrake.

When he got within a block of the inn, Clint circled around through the alleys and behind the nearby buildings to make sure that the last silent gunman wasn't skulking about in the shadows. Most of the area was filled with modest houses and a few of the smaller dry goods stores. It was getting to be past ten o'clock and all but a very few of the homes were dark. Every one of the stores had been locked up tight long ago.

The only noises Clint heard were echoes from one of the two saloon districts and even those were few and far between. Satisfied that there wasn't anyone in the immediate vicinity, Clint made a beeline back to the inn and circled it once more before heading to the only lower-level window that had a light burning behind it.

Someone was in the kitchen, which had its own side door

leading out to an alley. As Clint rapped on the rectangular window set in the door, he thought how nice it would be to walk down a street again and leave the alley-crawling to the cats.

The innkeeper's wary face edged into view. When he saw who was outside, he showed himself completely and smiled apologetically while unlocking the door.

"Sorry 'bout that," he said after Clint was inside. "Can't be too careful with the element we get in this town. I usually keep the front door unlocked, but I heard gunshots while I was out earlier and—"

Clint interrupted with a raised hand. "Never hurts to be too careful. Nothing happened over here did it?"

"No, no, no," the innkeeper blustered. "It was closer to Main Street. This is an older part of town and keeps pretty quiet. Lots of families from when this town was half its size. School's right down the street . . ."

Clint ignored the rest of the man's prattling and helped himself to one of the biscuits that was in the breadbox on the table. It was hard enough to have been left over from two dinners ago, but he ate it down just the same. A pitcher of water sat next to the breadbox, and it helped get the rest of the pasty bread off the top of his mouth.

The innkeeper joined him. "Help yourself. I was just getting a little snack."

"What about the ladies I checked in earlier? Have they left?"

"No, they're upstairs. I sent up some whiskey to one of their rooms. She seemed fairly . . . vocal about getting something more to drink than water."

That would be Maddy.

"Has anyone been to see them?" Clint asked.

"No, sir."

"Good. I'm about set to turn in, myself."

"Care for another?" the innkeeper asked, holding out another of the rock-hard biscuits.

"No thanks. My teeth aren't strong enough."

Shrugging, the innkeeper waited for Clint to leave before chucking the biscuits out the door, where they could choke some of the tomcats who'd been keeping him up nights.

FORTY

Most of the light downstairs was coming from the kitchen. Clint fumbled his way in the dark until he found the old staircase that led up to the rooms. The inn felt more like one of the bigger homes in the area that had been renovated to act as a business. Upstairs, there were only five doors. The one he'd rented for Maddy was closest to the stairs, and he'd learned Greta's was down at the end of the hall when he'd checked Maddy in.

Clint knocked a few times on Maddy's door and got no answer. He tried a few more times before he started getting nervous. Drawing his gun, he tried the door, found it unlocked, and opened it slowly.

She was curled up on her bed with her back to the door. A half-empty bottle of whiskey was on the floor. Clint holstered his weapon and snuck up to her side. It took several good shakes to wake her up, and when she came around, there was only a faint glimmer of consciousness in her eyes.

"It's me, Clint."

She grunted and rubbed her eyes. Her breath smelled of the cheap liquor, but she looked more tired than drunk. "Clint? I . . ."

"I want you to lock the door after me. Understand?"

She nodded and got groggily to her feet. When he left her room and pulled the door shut, Clint waited until he heard the latch fall into place before heading to Greta's room. He tried that door and couldn't get it to budge. Good girl.

Knocking, he said quietly, "Open up, Greta. It's Clint."

He heard footsteps behind the door and saw the handle start to turn. "Who'd you say it was?" she asked cautiously.

"A big fan of your special dessert."

He could hear her laughing as she worked the latch and opened the door. After he walked in, she twisted the little knob over the door handle. "I thought I heard shooting earlier," she said while Clint checked the windows and made sure the shades were drawn. "Are you all right?"

Standing away from the window, Clint looked as though he didn't know what to do with himself when there wasn't a crisis that needed solving. Finally, he dropped himself onto the bed and tossed his hat to the floor. "Styles sent for those gunmen, and they were scouring the town for Scotelli on their way to your place. I took care of three of them."

Just then, Greta noticed the blood on Clint's shirt and rushed toward him. "You were hit?" she asked while tugging his shirt open.

Clint had put that out of his mind, but when he was reminded of the wound, he felt a slight pinching pain. "It's just a scratch," he said. "I think the bleeding's stopped."

It had stopped, but it had also dried so that his shirt was plastered to the wound. When Greta removed the clothing, fresh blood began seeping from a wound that looked more like a claw mark left by an animal than a bullet wound. It raked along his ribs from front to back, but wasn't even deep enough to require stitches.

Greta dropped his short to the floor and picked up a small folded towel that had been lying upon a dresser. She dipped it in the washbasin and pressed the wet material against Clint's side, looking into his eyes as he drew in a quick breath. "Did I hurt you?" she asked.

"No, it feels good to have someone taking care of me."

She smiled and tended to the rough scratch. In a few minutes, she'd torn up the towel and wrapped it around his torso. There was only enough material to go around him twice, but it was plenty to cover the wound. When she was finished, Greta wiped her forehead and sat on the edge of the bed.

"I'm so tired, Clint. Tired of running and tired of being pushed around by someone that was supposed to be taking orders from me. Will this be over soon?"

Clint nodded. "With Styles locked up for now and Scotelli on his way to jail, all there is to worry about is that last gunman. I couldn't find him, but I know he's still around. From what I saw, they weren't the type to leave before their job is done."

"Come here," she whispered while patting the space next to her on the mattress. "I want you close to me."

Clint eased himself down onto the bed. Its thin mattress was only slightly better than sleeping on the ground, especially when compared to the accommodations at either one of the deluxe saloons in town. Still, Greta was more than enough to distract him when she loosened her hair and let it fall in a golden cascade over her shoulders.

Reaching over to the bedside table, she turned down the lamp until there was just enough light in the room to see by. The shadows grew all around them, which seemed to put Greta more at ease.

She stood with her back to him and looked out the window. "So there's still someone out there?" she asked quietly.

"Yes, but I don't think he'll know to look here for you. I doubt even Styles would have an idea where we are."

Running her fingers along the edge of the window, Greta turned to face him and held her hands up to her neck. Slowly, she ran her fingertips down her body, gently over the front of her dress, and stopped at her waist. "But you'll protect me," she stated sincerely. "I feel so safe when you're close by."

She took a step toward him and put her hands on his shoulders. When she looked down at him, her hair fell around his face, allowing Clint to breathe in the rose-scented perfume she always wore. "I want you closer," she whispered. "Make love to me."

Clint stood up and held her in his arms. She felt warm and supple, melting into his embrace as if her body had been molded onto his. She eased him out of his pants as his hands were busy unbuttoning her dress. Naked, she looked like a vision from a dream with the soft light playing over the slopes of her figure. When she pushed him back onto the bed, it felt much more comfortable than he'd remembered.

FORTY-ONE

Greta stretched out on the bed, her back arching so that her full, soft breasts caught what little light there was. Her nipples stood erect and pointing toward the ceiling, and she moaned softly in anticipation of his next move. Clint crawled next to her and lay on his side. He wanted to take his time and feel her body respond to his touch. Even in the dim light, he could see the golden thatch of hair between her legs and how it parted when she opened her knees, as if to invite him inside.

For the moment, Clint resisted the temptation and instead brushed aside the hair that had fallen in front of her face. He moved his fingertips to tickle the back of her neck and moved in closer until he could start nibbling on her earlobe.

Greta smiled widely and closed her eyes. She squirmed on the bed and clutched the sheets in her hands. The leg farthest from Clint came up close to her body, pushing until she was on her side facing him. When his teeth gently pressed into the skin of her neck, she rolled onto her back and reached out to run her fingers down his back.

"That's nice," she purred while reaching out with her other hand to trace a line over his chest.

Clint playfully bit her neck and shoulders and worked his way down to her breasts. When his lips brushed against her nipples, Greta grabbed the back of Clint's head with both hands and pressed him against her. A low moan issued from deep in her throat. Her flesh tasted sweet and salty, her natural flavor mixed in with the sweaty excitement of the moment.

She wriggled beneath him as he worked on her. One of her breasts fit perfectly in hand while his mouth wrapped around another. His tongue ran between them and then over her finely rounded curves. At first, he took quick tastes with flicks of his tongue. Her nipples, which were normally small and pink, were now hard as little candies.

Clint pressed his lips around a tight, pert little mound and kissed it. She stroked the back of his neck, her grip tightening as he began sucking it. When he pressed the sensitive pink nub between his teeth, she squealed in pleasure, her eyes growing wide. Then his tongue ran the smooth valley between her breasts and began tasting the other one.

By the time his mouth was brushing the contours of her stomach, Clint could feel the excitement building up within her, tightening her muscles beneath his mouth. Before he could get his face between her legs, she moved out from under him and crawled forward on hands and knees.

They met toward the foot of the bed, both of them on their knees facing each other. She let him smooth her hair back as her hands felt their way down his body. She was careful of his wound and seemed fascinated by the numerous scars that he'd collected. Starting at the gouge in his neck, she kissed every imperfection as her strong hands worked the muscles of his back.

They maneuvered around the mattress until he was able to lie back, and she was kneeling astride him. Now it was her turn to taste his skin, which she did with an eager appetite. She nibbled here and there, lingering in some places while quickly tasting others. The farther down she got, the less she seemed like the proper and demure Greta Ulrich that he'd come to know.

She nipped at his chest, playfully bringing him a twinge of pain, which made the feel of her warm tongue all the better. Then, trailing her fingernails over his shoulders and chest, she worked her way down his body, darting her little tongue until she was looking straight down at the hardening flesh between his legs.

With a shake of her head, Greta draped her hair over Clint's stomach so he couldn't see where her mouth was headed next. At first, the gentle tickle of her soft hair on his skin was pleasure enough. Then he felt a quick kiss on his thigh, followed by the brush of lips at the base of his penis.

Her tongue sent chills through him as it tasted his pole from top to bottom in one stroke. Clint wanted to reach forward and move her hair so he could see her face, but before he could get hold of her, Greta swallowed his entire member and vigorously sucked his pole while grabbing tightly onto his hips with both hands.

Her head bobbed up and down, filling the room with the wet sound of her mouth at work. When she had him completely in her throat, she pressed her lips tightly together. As she moved her head up, her tongue caressed his shaft until she was able to swirl it around the head of his cock. Then her lips closed around him and sucked on the tip until he thought the sensations were about to overwhelm him.

Clint didn't know he was making any sound at all until a knock came on the door, interrupting him in the middle of a throaty groan.

Greta looked up with her hair all but hiding her face. "Did somebody track us down?" she asked in a hushed voice.

"One way to find out," Clint said as he got up and took his gun from the holster on the floor. He walked across the room and listened at the door just as the knock came again. The sound was light and quick, like a bird pecking on the wood.

With his gun at the ready, Clint stood to the side and said, "Who's there?"

"Just open up, will you?" It was Maddy's voice, still a little blurred from sleep.

"Is something wrong?"

"Open the door," she said insistently.

Clint did and stepped aside to let her in and closed the door behind her. Dressed in a plain white slip and holding a candlestick, Maddy walked in and looked at the bed. Greta was leaning forward under the covers, holding a sheet up to cover herself. Then Maddy looked at Clint, who was naked with a gun in his hand.

"Caught you two at a good time I see." Maddy said mischievously.

Clint set the pistol down next to his holster and picked up his pants. "There had better be someone on their way up here with their fingers on the trigger . . ."

"Not quite." Sitting on the edge of the bed, Maddy flicked a stray piece of black hair from her eyes. "It's kinda hard to sleep with you two carrying on in here, though. Especially with me all alone in my room. I get scared, too, you know."

Grudgingly, Clint said, "I guess you can sleep here tonight."

Maddy looked over at Greta, who seemed as much aroused as she was embarrassed with having been caught in the act. Then she looked at Clint who was hiking his pants up.

"No need to get dressed on my account," Maddy said. "We all want some comfort tonight." Standing up, she moved the thin straps of her slip off her shoulders and let the filmy material drop to her feet. She leaned over to blow out her candle, giving Clint a perfect view of her body's profile: large, full breasts swinging slowly with her movement; plump, rounded backside jutting out toward the bed.

When the room was back to its original state of dim light, Maddy turned to Clint and placed her hands on his sides, carefully running them down and hooking her thumbs in the waistband of his jeans. She pulled them off in one motion and dropped to her knees in front of him. Her lips pursed into a red bow, which ran over his shaft as it sprung back to life. She sucked him just as loudly as Greta had been doing moments ago, and when she pulled her head back to hold his swollen tip between her teeth, she looked over at Greta, who was watching every move with guilty interest.

Maddy stood, took Clint's hand, and led him onto the bed. She sat next to him with Greta on the other side. "We both owe you our lives," Maddy said. "We both want you tonight. I don't see why we both can't have you."

Before anyone could say another word, Maddy pressed Clint's back down to the mattress and crawled next to him. Hesitantly, Greta watched as Maddy nibbled on Clint's neck while fondling her large breasts with her own hands. She tweaked her nipples while Clint was getting more and more aroused.

From where she was sitting, Greta could see his cock growing so hard that it stood straight up. It was swollen to its full size, and she couldn't think of anything else besides feeling that inside of her. She wanted him so much that she quickly got past the strangeness of having another woman in her bed and climbed up on top of Clint to satisfy her urgent desire.

When Greta felt him beneath her, she closed her eyes and reached down to guide his shaft between her legs. Her thighs were so moist that he glided effortlessly into her as she eased herself down until his head was buried up inside her body, pressing against every tender spot she had. The excitement made her weak, and she leaned forward to hold on to him for support.

Her hands felt the muscles of his abdomen below her and when she opened her eyes, she found Maddy laying on her side with her legs spread open. She gripped the back of Clint's head as he buried his face in her sex. Maddy's smile was one of blind ecstasy. She grit her teeth and grunted like an animal as her hips bucked up against him, pushing his tongue deep inside.

Greta couldn't take her eyes off of his tongue as it worked between Maddy's pink, wet lips. When she saw the other woman lean her head back as Clint drank her juices like a man in a desert, Greta found herself bucking her hips harder and harder.

Clint had felt bad at first for indulging himself with Maddy. But when he felt Greta climb on top and impale herself on him, he started thrusting his hips up in time to her rhythm until his body was slapping deliciously against hers. Meanwhile, Maddy couldn't get enough of him tasting her, and she started moaning loudly with her head tossed back and her hair whipping from side to side.

When he was on the verge of climax, Clint felt Greta's weight move off of him and Maddy pull away from his face. He looked up just in time to see Maddy's plump buttocks centering over his groin. She straddled him and eased down until his slick rod was buried deep between her thighs. Maddy sat straight up and leaned her head back again, letting the ends of her hair brush along the upper slope of her backside.

Greta appeared at his side and kissed him hungrily on the mouth. Her tongue played with his, and her hands vigorously rubbed Clint's chest. Soon, she sat on top of him with one knee on either side of his head. She straightened her back and held on to the posts at the top of the bed. Clint looked up to see the slick dampness between her legs, shimmering over him like a pot of honey.

Laughing deeply from the back of her throat, Greta lowered her vagina on to his lips, only to pull it away a second later. Overcome with the feeling of Maddy thrusting down onto his shaft and Greta so close to his mouth, Clint reached up and grabbed hold of Greta's tight buttocks and pulled them down until his mouth was buried between her legs.

They went on all night. If there were any other guests in the hotel, they wouldn't have been able to sleep. The innkeeper tried several times to get them to quiet down, but not one of the threesome could hear him knocking.

FORTY-TWO

Nolan was a patient man. He had to be in order to stay alive and not make mistakes in his business. He'd been just starting his second drink when he heard the gunshots outside. There were too many for it to be the sound of his own men doing their jobs, which meant it was either not anything to do with his men or that someone was shooting back at them. He'd checked it out and within a few minutes had found the bodies.

Three of his crew down and no others. It could only have been Clint Adams that had taken his three. Judging by the tracks and blood drops, his men had done some damage . . . but not enough.

Having seen that, Nolan went back to the Three Aces and saw Adams climbing up the stairs for the hotel rooms. He'd waited a few minutes and didn't hear anything. He'd gone upstairs himself and found the bouncers standing right where they should have been. He'd looked toward the bouncer at Styles's door—the one he'd paid off—and got a nod toward the end of the hall.

Nolan had checked every inch of this place a few days before his men had arrived and knew that last door was a back stairway leading to an alley. Adams had been here to look and nothing else before scooting out the back.

Turning casually toward the main stairs, Nolan went back

down to the saloon proper and found his table. His drink was untouched. He sat back down and waited.

That was seven hours ago.

The sun was beginning to peek through the saloon's front windows, and the bouncers had changed shifts. The one in Nolan's pocket nodded again and shrugged on his way out.

"Ain't heard a peep," the big man said as he went out the door.

Nolan figured as much. If there was a peep to be heard, he would have heard it already. There was still one piece missing. Still one more of his men left unaccounted for. Easing down into his chair, Nolan ordered breakfast and waited for that man to report in. If he didn't come before he was finished eating, he would go and look for him.

He thought for a second about finding his men dead. About The Gunsmith executing his professional killers like they were nothing. Then the waitress came, and he ordered his food. Tomorrow, he would order some new men just as easily.

Kenneth Styles had lost most of the feeling in his legs hours ago. His hands were going numb, but he worked his fingers to keep the blood flowing since he knew he would be a free man at any moment. Like any smart deal maker, Styles had a backup plan that would take care of everything. All he had to do was sit back and wait for Nolan to get him out. Then he would go to the funerals of Madeline Lowell and Greta Ulrich and squeeze out a few tears in his new saloons.

He'd fallen asleep sometime in the early morning. He couldn't see a clock, but the noises downstairs were tapering off, which meant it was getting close to dawn. Styles let his head slump forward, and before he knew it, he was out. When he woke up, his hands and feet were still tied. He was still in the same room, looking at the same door, listening to the same heavy feet shuffling outside. That meant something was wrong.

Styles shifted in his chair, trying to get enough slack in his ropes so he could get a look out the window. Over the previous night, he'd been able to work the knots loose a little, but not enough to give him much hope. Now all he wanted was to look behind him. After a few minutes of struggling, he managed to turn his body less than half an inch. Exasperated, he took in what he could see.

The furniture was moved to the sides of the room and the door. Some of the shadows were starting to fade, which meant that morning was on its way. There wasn't much left for him to do besides wait and hope that Nolan hadn't left him.

Having found the bodies of his partners, the fourth of Nolan's men spent the night searching for the ones who'd put them on their backs. The corpses had been stuffed out of sight, but the killer knew where to look. Normally, it was he who hid the bodies, which gave him an extra edge in finding them.

He didn't want to go back to Nolan and tell him about the others being killed if he didn't at least have one body of his own to hand over in return. Scotelli's would have done, but he was gone. The killer knew Scotelli was nowhere near good enough to pull a trigger faster than those three, which meant there was someone else. And try as he might, he couldn't find the one responsible.

Mandrake was a big town with lots of places to hole up. He'd spent the rest of the night looking, but came up empty.

By the time dawn had broken, the shooter decided to head back to the Three Aces and tell Nolan about what he'd found. Hell, Nolan probably knew all about it anyway.

With his eyes still open and searching for any sign of his targets, the fourth man walked amid the townspeople, who were just starting to poke their heads out for another day.

Inside the Three Aces, Nolan sat at his table, sopping up a puddle of sausage gravy from an otherwise empty plate in front of him. His head craned up slowly to watch the last of his men approach the table. Steam rose in front of him from a large copper mug.

Nolan waited until his man was sitting down before breaking the silence. "Coffee?" he said, pointing toward the mug.

The fourth man nodded.

Nolan waved down a serving girl and ordered the drink. The table was enveloped in a deathly silence until the second mug arrived and the server had left.

"I know about the others," Nolan said. "Now tell me something I don't know."

The coffee was good. Hot and strong. It was the icy tone in his boss's voice, however, that woke the fourth man up more than anything else. "Whoever did the shooting was good. The others put up a fight, but they were just overwhelmed. More likely it was an ambush."

"No, you were right the first time. There was only one man. I saw him come back here after the smoke had cleared. It was Clint Adams."

The last shooter nodded gravely and took another sip of coffee. "What about Styles? Is he still up there?"

"Yeah. That horse's ass can't seem to keep himself from getting hog-tied. I'm startin' to think he likes the feel of the ropes."

"We still going to get him out?"

Nolan sighed and popped the last chunk of biscuit into his mouth. "I was hopin' that Adams would show up before we tipped our hand. Maybe take him by surprise. There's plenty of ways to get rich by killin' a man like that. We wait too long, though, and this place'll get too crowded. Hell, too many folks are starting to come in here already."

"Were you here all night?"

"Pretty much." Suddenly Nolan threw his napkin onto the table and swore under his breath. "This job should've been over yesterday," he seethed. "Did you find any trace of Adams or those two ladies?"

The fourth man shook his head. "No. But they could be anywhere. I didn't figure it would be smart to start kicking down doors."

Nolan thought for a few seconds and pushed his chair away from the table. "Hell with it. Let's get Styles and get out of here. We'll come back for the women. Should be easier without that banker gettin' under our feet anyway." Nolan strode purposefully toward the staircase. He didn't have to look behind him to know his partner would be there.

Both men wore their grim, stony faces. Their feet clomped on the floorboards. It didn't matter if anyone heard them coming because only an act of God could stop them.

FORTY-THREE

Clint woke up the next morning with Greta in his arms. She was curled up tight against him and sleeping soundly. She stirred slightly when he crept out from under the covers, and she finally opened her eyes by the time he got dressed.

"Where are you going?" she asked.

"There's still plenty to take care of out there, unless you've forgotten about those men with the guns that are after you."

Sitting up with her back against the wall behind the bed, Greta stretched her arms and let the sheet drop away from her naked body. "I want to check on my saloon."

Clint pulled on his boots and strapped his gun around his waist. "Absolutely not. I'll check on both places, but you need to stay here with Maddy. You two should be safe as long as you don't show yourselves."

"I won't hide here forever."

"Just today," Clint said as he sat down on the bed next to her. "After today, all of this will be over."

Before she could reply, he kissed her on the lips and walked out the door. He was about to knock before entering Maddy's room, but her door swung open just as he was raising his fist. Maddy stood there wearing the slip she'd had on last night. Even through the whiskey in her system, she managed to look more awake than Greta and seemed even more alert than Clint felt.

"Heavy steps there, big fella," she said with a wink. "Heard you coming down the hall."

"Same as last night I suppose?"

That brought about the first blush he'd ever seen on Maddy's face. Until now, Clint had hardly thought anything could bring about a response like that from her. She stepped aside and waved him in.

"No time," Clint said without stepping from the hall. "I just wanted to tell you to stay here and make sure Greta does the same."

"Where would we go? I'm not all that quick with a gun."

"Just keep an eye on her. I'll come and get you when it's over."

"It'll be over today?" she asked hopefully.

Clint nodded. "I've had enough of this. It ends now one way or the other."

"How will I know if you're okay?"

"If I don't come for you by sundown, you'll know I'm pretty far from okay."

Clint could hear the gunshots just as he walked through the front door of the Three Aces Saloon. There were people already running outside, and when he stepped into the main room, he already had his gun drawn and ready.

All he could see were people making their way toward him. Stepping away from the door, Clint let the crowd pass, which was made up mainly of townspeople who'd been waiting for their breakfasts. The hardier crowd wouldn't be in till later, which explained why they were running for the door instead of standing guard over their drinks and poker chips when the shooting had started.

Clint scanned the room for any of the steely eyed gunmen he'd seen outside the boardinghouse. All the while he headed toward the stairs in back, knowing full well where the shooting was coming from and what it was about. He only hoped he wasn't too late to keep some of the bouncers from getting themselves killed.

He ran up the stairs and dove to the floor as soon as he got to the top. A bullet whipped over his head and chewed into the wall behind him. Laying flat on his stomach, Clint rolled to the side to get a clear shot, stopping once he caught sight of the man in simple clothing staring down the hall with cold, dead eyes.

Those eyes had become beacons to Clint and caught his attention immediately. Ignoring everything else, Clint used those beacons to take his shot. The pistol bucked in his hand, but Clint's target had already moved. Clint used the spare moment to get to his feet and take in the scene.

A body lie sprawled on the floor. It was a huge man wrapped in an ill-fitting black vest. One of the bouncers, but not one that Clint recognized. There should have been at least two more of the guards.

More shots echoed from Styles's room, and Clint was already there with his back pressed against the wall next to the door frame. Not wanting to see another of the bouncers die, Clint ignored every bit of common sense he had and swung himself around the door frame and into the room.

He first saw the killers. There had only been four at the boardinghouse, and he'd killed three of them. Seeing two alive in the room meant there were more in town than Clint had thought. That was not good.

Styles was out of his ropes and on his feet. His eyes were darting crazily about the room as if he'd soaked up all the fire and emotion that his killers lacked. He held a lantern in one hand and looked as though he was about to throw it at the closest person he could find.

As soon as Clint had cleared the door, both of the killers' guns were aimed at him. They didn't fire, however. Instead, they looked back toward Styles, who had lowered the lantern but kept it firmly in hand.

For a few seconds, everyone froze. The other two bouncers were armed and holding their guns out in front of them with fear in their eyes. They weren't experienced shooters, but they had the room covered, which might have been enough to get a lucky shot. The killers didn't seem concerned with them, however. They knew the bouncers would be dead as soon as they wanted them dead and were focusing in on Clint.

"Get out of here," Clint told the bouncers without looking away from those cold eyes. "Go get the sheriff."

The young men in black vests, for all their size, seemed

more than willing to get out of the cramped room. One of them took a step toward the door, causing one of the killers to bend his wrist just enough to shift his aim and pull the trigger.

Clint had seen that coming and was already in motion before the hammer dropped. With one hand, he pulled the bouncer by his vest and shoved him through the door. Luckily, the killer had been aiming for a head shot, otherwise he couldn't have missed the bouncer's huge frame. As it was, Clint was fast enough to get the bouncer moving so the slug could dig into the wall rather than the young man's skull.

As soon as the bouncer was out the door, Clint returned fire. He ducked low and to the side to avoid the next round of lead as both killers sent bullets in his direction. The shots were clean and precise. The first ripped through Clint's sleeve while he was stepping out of the way and the second would have struck flesh if Clint hadn't been able to send his own round into the shooter's chest as the man with the cold eyes was firing.

His round hit the last of the men that Clint had spotted outside the boardinghouse, pulling the killer's aim off center and sending the bullet meant for Clint into the ceiling. Even in death, the shooter's face showed no emotion. Instead, he seemed as if he'd died long ago and was just waiting for someone to push him over.

When the body fell beside him, Nolan was too busy to notice.

"Shoot him! Shoot him!" Styles screamed.

Clint watched the remaining gunman's face for any sign of what was going on inside the man's head.

Nolan wore a mask of granite and then . . . he blinked.

Jumping on the fleeting glimpse of humanity in the killer, Clint stood tall and turned his gun to cover the man next to Styles. "You want to die along with the rest of your men," Clint warned, "then you just let me know."

Behind Clint, the other bouncer had made tracks out the door, leaving him alone with Styles, Nolan, and a warm corpse.

The businessman screamed at the shooter he'd hired, but got no response. Finally, he threw down the lantern and the room filled with the stench of kerosene. "Guess I'll have to finish this myself," he said as he pulled a metal container from his pocket.

"What the hell do you think you're doing?" Nolan asked.

Clint was surprised more at hearing the killer's voice than at what Styles had done. He watched as the gunman turned on his employer, noticing that his aim didn't waver an inch.

Nolan glared at Styles while still preparing himself to fire on Clint. The businessman seemed as if he'd lost his mind and stood in the flammable puddle as if the kerosene was nothing but rain water.

"Seems like nobody wants to do their jobs!" Styles yelled. "You can't even seem to kill two women without losing all of your men in the process."

Clint heard footsteps from the hall and spotted Sheriff Cole in the corner of his eye. Before he could stop him, the portly lawman stepped into the room and started pulling his gun.

"All right, everyone," Cole announced, "drop your weapons and come outside."

Nolan barely acknowledged the sheriff was even there. He was too busy watching Styles as the man dropped to his knees and snatched the gun from the dead killer's hand. Once he was armed, Styles took shaky aim at Clint and then the sheriff while fumbling with the container in his other hand.

"Why are you just standing there, Nolan?" Styles ranted as he opened the container. Matches fell from the small rectangular tin. He grabbed one and started scratching it along one of the tin's rough edges. A spark ignited on the match as well as in the businessman's eyes.

"I told her!" Styles screamed. "This place is mine or I'd burn it down just like I did all the others!"

Two gunshots exploded in the room. One was a bullet that blew Styles back against a wall as he reflexively flicked his match toward the ground. When the stick hit the floor, Styles was waiting for the whoosh of flames and the heat that he hadn't felt since he'd turned the town of Wayne into ashes.

Instead, there was just the sound of wood lightly tapping on wood.

Clint was holding his breath. He didn't let it out until he was certain his own bullet had found its mark. Sure enough, the matchstick that hit the kerosene had been cut neatly in half, its spark snuffed out by the lead from Clint's gun.

Styles looked like he didn't know what to think. The tapping he heard was still coming and was becoming a steady rhythm. When he looked down, he felt the first bite of pain in his chest. His blood dripped from a hole in his shirt and tapped against the floor until his body toppled over to land in a twitching heap.

Nolan held his pistol in hand, the barrel still smoking after blowing a hole through Styles's heart. He looked at the sheriff and then at Clint. Both had their guns pointed at him.

Tossing his weapon onto Styles's chest, Nolan held his hands out to either side. "Crazy men got no part in this business," he said. "I'd rather take my chances with fate." Then, quicker than Clint had thought it possible for a man to move, Nolan pitched himself out the window and onto the narrow balcony outside.

Both men fired after him, but not before Nolan cleared the wooden railing and landed on the street below.

FORTY-FOUR

Clint stood in front of the Three Aces, holding Greta's hands. As much as he wanted to stay for a while longer, he couldn't get himself to walk inside that place again.

"I could use someone like you around here," she said.

"What for? Do you plan on getting into trouble like this again?"

"No," she said while turning her face away. "I just . . . I don't want you to leave. Mandrake isn't the worst place to settle down. And what if someone else tries to move in like Styles did?"

Clint brushed her cheek with the back of his hand. "I wouldn't worry about that. After what happened here, the word will spread like wildfire that this is a good place for a drink, but a bad place to pick a fight. Besides, Styles was crazy. Turns out he was even crazier than Scotelli."

"So it was Styles that set those fires?"

"Apparently. All the men he'd hired had plenty of blood on their hands, but Styles seemed to get a kick out of burning down his competition."

"What about Scotelli?" she asked. "And the other one that escaped? What about them?"

"I checked on Scotelli a few minutes ago. He died in his cell last night. Sheriff Cole didn't think the doctor needed to be bothered."

Greta's eyes turned cold as she stared up at the bright blue sky. "Guess his laziness finally paid off."

Guiding her face with a finger on her chin, Clint got her looking toward him again. "Don't worry about the other one. Most of those folks inside your place were standing in the street when he came out that window. They all saw him grab the first horse he could get his hands on and ride away. He's got no reason to come back here, Greta. He's a professional. You don't owe him any money, and you didn't cause him any harm. It would be a lot of trouble for nothing."

"You talk like you understand him."

"In a way, I do. I don't agree with what he does, but I understand it."

Greta stepped closer to him and slowly wrapped her arms around his waist. "You won't stay?"

Clint thought about the last thing he'd said about Nolan and how it applied just as well to himself at the moment. Rather than say that to Greta, he held her for a bit and kissed her softly on the lips.

"I'd like to," he said. "But I'd only have to leave sooner or later anyway. I've learned that, more often than not, sooner is better."

They stood in each other's embrace for a few more seconds before finally breaking apart.

On his way to the livery, Clint almost turned onto Third Street, but Maddy was already standing at the corner.

"Thought I'd save you a trip," she said when they met on the sidewalk in front of a bordello that would be closed until four that afternoon.

"I appreciate it. I wanted to get on the trail as soon as I could."

"You've got somewhere better to be than Mandrake?" she said with mock surprise. "This has become the murder capital of Iowa overnight. Plus, you've still got a room with your own personal maid." Her fingers worked their way over his body as if to show that she already knew every inch of him. "Not even one more day? I thought after last night you'd never want to leave."

Thinking about the breathless night he'd spent in a bed with

Maddy and Greta almost made him give in to her offer. "One more night like that, and I might not even be able to leave my room."

"So, where to now?"

"I need to go back to Wayne. There's some people that deserve to know that Styles and his men are out of the picture."

"I talked to Greta," Maddy said. "She told me how much she wanted you to stay as well. Said she might not even mind giving last night another try."

Clint couldn't keep the surprise from showing on his face. "That's the first I heard of that."

"She's not the type to talk like that in front of a man. Even one who knows her like you do. But don't get too full of yourself, 'cause that's not all we talked about." Turning to look back at the Prairie Dog Saloon, which could just be seen from where they were, Maddy beamed with a certain excited pride. "We both think that we could do all the expanding we wanted right here in Mandrake. If we pooled our resources, we could build both our places up and make them different enough to satisfy any taste that would come through here. Maybe then we could buy out a few places out of state . . . together."

"Sounds a lot easier than racing each other for it and splitting your money with the likes of Ken Styles."

"It does, doesn't it? This just feels right. If the other night proved anything," Maddy said in a sexy whisper, "it's that two women can drive any man out of his skull. That's more reliable than any gun."

Clint laughed and scooped Maddy up into his arms. "Next time I come through here, remind me to leave my valuables at the sheriff's office."

Maddy kicked her legs and put her lips against Clint's ear. "Next time you're here, you won't be leaving that room."

Setting her down, Clint started to say something, but was cut off by Maddy's deep, penetrating kiss. The spicy taste of her mixed with Greta's smooth sweetness. He knew that when they put their talents together professionally, they would be a force to be reckoned with.

"I'll see you, Maddy."

"Give us awhile. That way, you can see what me and Greta

have planned. Our new places will be as big as this whole town!"

Clint turned and headed for the livery. He knew both saloon owners would be fine. In fact, given a few years, one of them would probably be mayor.

Eclipse was raring to go and so was Clint by the time he got the anxious stallion saddled and loaded up. On his way out, he stopped in front of Arlen, who was in his usual spot, leaning his chair against the front of the old barn.

"How much do I owe you?" he asked the liveryman.

"Let's see . . ." Arlen clenched his eyes shut and drew numbers in the air. "Twenty dollars."

"What?"

"There's the stable fees, the food and fresh water, not to mention the damage your little gunfight did to my stables."

"Let me get this straight. I nearly get killed in there, and you want *me* to pay for the damages?"

Shrugging, Arlen said, "Business is business."

Watch for

BAYOU GHOSTS

235th novel in the exciting GUNSMITH series
from Jove

Coming in July!